OCEAN STATE

Also by Stewart O'nan

FICTION

Henry, Himself

City of Secrets

West of Sunset

The Odds

Emily, Alone

Songs for the Missing

Last Night at the Lobster

The Good Wife

The Night Country

Wish You Were Here

Everyday People

A Prayer for the Dying

A World Away

The Speed Queen

The Names of the Dead

Snow Angels

In the Walled City

NONFICTION

Faithful (with Stephen King)

The Circus Fire

The Vietnam Reader (editor)

On Writers and Writing by John Gardner (editor)

SCREENPLAY

Poe

OCEAN STATE

STEWART O'NAN

Atlantic Monthly Press
New York

FIRST EDITION

Published simultaneously in Canada
Printed in the United States of America

First Grove Atlantic hardcover edition: March 2022

This book was set in 12.5-pt. Bembo Std
by Alpha Design & Composition of Pittsfield, NH.

Library of Congress Cataloging-in-Publication data is available for this title.

ISBN 978-0-8021-5927-4
eISBN 978-0-8021-5928-1

Atlantic Monthly Press
an imprint of Grove Atlantic
154 West 14th Street
New York, NY 10011

Distributed by Publishers Group West

groveatlantic.com

22 23 24 25 10 9 8 7 6 5 4 3 2 1

For Angel Olsen

Hi-Five.

Sometimes our enemies
are closer than we think

Angel Olsen

Shut up kiss me hold me tight

Angel Olsen

In the House by the Line & Twine

When I was in eighth grade my sister helped kill another girl. She was in love, my mother said, like it was an excuse. She didn't know what she was doing. I had never been in love then, not really, so I didn't know what my mother meant, but I do now.

This was in Ashaway, Rhode Island, outside Westerly, down along the shore. That fall we lived in a house by the river, across the road from the mill where my grandmother had met my grandfather. The Line & Twine was closed, posted with rusty NO TRESPASSING signs, but just above the dam someone had snipped a hole in the fence with bolt cutters so you could sneak in the back. We used to roller-skate up and down the aisles between the dusty looms, Angel weaving, teaching me how to do crossovers and go backwards. She could do spins like an ice-skater, her hands making shapes in the air. I wanted to do spins and be graceful like her, but I was chubby and a klutz and when I stood beside her in church I was invisible. My mother said I shouldn't worry, that in time I'd find my special talent. "I was a late bloomer," she said, as if that was supposed to be comforting. What if I didn't have a special talent? I wanted to ask. What if a hopeless nerd was all I'd ever be?

My mother's talent was finding new boyfriends and new places for us to live. She worked as a nurse's aide at the Elms, an old folks' home in Westerly where my great-aunt Mildred lived, and didn't make any money. Fridays she'd come home and change, brushing her hair out, making up her face, using too much perfume. She'd been a cheerleader and could dance. She dieted, or tried to. Facing the narrow mirror on her closet, she complained that nothing fit her anymore. I used to look like you, she told Angel, like a threat, and it was true, in her old pictures they could have been twins. If she'd wanted to, she said, she could have married a doctor, but they were all assholes. Your father was sweet.

We knew our father was sweet. What we didn't understand was when he'd become an asshole, or why. My grandmother had never liked him because his family was Portuguese. He'd tricked my mother into turning Catholic and then abandoned her. Never trust a Port-a-gees, she said, like it was a joke. I had his dark hair and eyes, so what did that make me?

My mother's boyfriends tried to be sweet, but they were strangers. Sometimes they paid our rent and sometimes we split it. When they broke up with my mother—suddenly, drunkenly, their shouting jerking us from sleep—we would have to move again. Like her, we were always rooting for things to work out, far beyond where we should have. Our father was gone, and our mother couldn't stop wanting to be in love. "I swear this is the last time," she'd say, dead sober, and a month later she'd bring home another loser. They seemed to be getting younger and scruffier, which Angel thought was a bad sign. My mother didn't seem to notice. In the beginning, everything was new. She lost weight and kissed us too much and made promises she couldn't keep.

The last had been a deckhand named Wes who brought home lobsters and called her "Care" and took us to Block Island to ride bikes, until one night he smashed her phone when she tried to call the cops on him. Neither of them was bleeding, so the cops didn't charge anyone. "You guys are useless," my mother said. "Yeah," one of them said, "that's why we're here at one in the morning, cause we got nothing better to do." We were living in the top half of a duplex, and the next morning while Wes was out dragging the Sound, the three of us lugged everything we could carry down the stairs and shoved it in my mother's car.

The house by the Line & Twine was for sale, but in 2009 no one was going to buy it. My grandmother had worked in accounting with the owners, snowbirds who'd shipped off to Florida long before the Crash. Like most of the houses on River Road, it had been sitting empty for years. There was moss on the shingles and weeds in the gutters.

My grandmother came over to help us clean the kitchen. She brought her rubber gloves. "It's not the Taj Mahal," she said.

"It's fine," my mother said, as if we wouldn't be there long. "Angel Lynn. Quit with the face."

"I didn't say anything," she said, scowling.

"You don't have to."

I didn't say anything. I hardly ever said anything, afraid of making things worse. I watched them like a scorekeeper, silently recording every slight and insult, every failure to be kind. I was thirteen, and like all children, had an overdeveloped sense of justice. I wanted everyone to be happy, despite our actual lives.

At the duplex, Angel and I had shared a bedroom. Here we each had our own, our doors closed. Lying in bed, I missed her texting with her friends long after I'd stopped reading, the glow on her face as she concentrated soothing as a nightlight. My secret wish was that when I started high school I would magically turn into her, that I would inherit her powers, not just her looks and toughness but the confidence that attracted people to her, the knowledge that no matter what, she would always be wanted. Now, without her, in the dark, with the road silent and the river spilling over the dam behind the Line & Twine, that dream seemed even more unreachable.

Our father hadn't completely abandoned us. He still came by to do repairs like fixing the doorbell or snaking the shower drain, a constant problem with our long hair. He had us every second weekend, taking us surfcasting, letting us drive his truck on the beach. The summer people were gone, the mansions where he did landscaping shuttered for the season, their spiked iron gates chained. The clam shacks and Del's Lemonade stands were closed, and we'd end up in town for lunch at One Fish Two Fish, a grease pit in an old Burger King where we'd gone when we were little. It still had the original bright yellow-and-orange Formica booths, the tabletops chipped and dirty at the edges, every stray grain of salt visible. We didn't have a lot to say to one another, as if we were afraid of giving away secrets that might be used against us. We talked about school mostly, and Angel's job at CVS. He had an apartment in Pawcatuck over a Chinese restaurant, the whole place saturated with the smell of burnt cooking oil. He had to move the heavy sea chest he used as a coffee table to set up the pullout couch from Bob's he'd bought just for us, the same faded Little Mermaid sheets every time, though we'd long outgrown Ariel. Sunday, while my mother and grandmother were at church, we slept late and he made us waffles, another leftover from our childhood, before delivering us home. In our driveway, letting us out, he gave us each a twenty, as if tipping us. For our mother, sometimes he had a check and sometimes he didn't, depending on how business was. They fought bitterly over money, which embarrassed us, and it was a good weekend when he had the full payment. I stayed on the porch to wave him away while our mother and Angel went inside.

"How was it?" our mother asked. "What did you all do?"

"Nothing," we said. "The usual."

She wasn't really interested, and we were already searching for clues to what she'd done with her weekend, sniffing the air for any hint of weed or body spray, checking the ashtrays for Marlboro butts, the recycling bin for extra beer bottles.

One Sunday, Angel found the foil corner of a condom wrapper under our mother's nightstand. She showed it to me on the palm of her hand like evidence.

"So what?" I pretended I wasn't frightened by the idea of another stranger taking over our home.

"So she's fucking someone."

"Der."

"She was probably fucking drunk. She probably didn't even know the guy. I'm so grossed out right now. She's such a fucking skank."

I wanted to defend our mother. She was lonely and didn't know what else to do. "At least he's not still here."

"Just wait," Angel said, and she was right.

The next Friday our mother warned us that Russ was coming to pick her up. He was a fireman but also had a landscaping business. We expected him to have a truck like our father, but the car that pulled up was a little silver Honda like our grandmother's. Russ was shorter than our mother, and bald, with thick bifocals and a salt-and-pepper beard and a gut that stuck out over his belt. Instead of skinny jeans and motorcycle boots, he wore forest-green corduroys and brown loafers. He had a chunky class ring, and shook our hands limply, like Reverend Ochs after church. Our mother made a point of saying they were going out to dinner, then to a movie at the Stonington Regal, as if they hadn't met at a bar.

"Weird," Angel said as we watched them drive off.

"Yeah."

"He's like Papa Smurf."

"That's mean," I said.

"Oh Carol, I want to put my smurf in your smurf. I'm going to smurf you all smurf smurf."

I slapped her on the shoulder and we laughed, bumping into each other like teammates.

"Oh my God," she said. "What if he's the one?"

"Stop."

"It's sad, actually. It's like she's giving up."

"He's not that bad," I said, because I thought she was still joking, but when I looked at her she was wiping away tears.

"Ange, come on."

She turned her back so I wouldn't see and reached for a tissue, blew. She hated to cry, thinking it made her weak, but she cried all the time. "It's so fucked-up. She's just going to make it worse. You make a mistake, you fix it, you don't make it again, you know?"

"Yeah," I said, but I was too frightened to admit I didn't know what we were talking about anymore. Her boyfriend Myles, I guessed, because normally Angel would be with him, the two of them cocooned in their own little world. By the time I realized what she meant, it was too late.

The girl my sister helped kill was named Birdy Alves. On the news they called her Beatriz, but everyone at school called her Birdy. She played soccer and softball and worked at the D'Angelo on Granite Street. She was petite, with big eyes and a heart-shaped face. Like Angel, she was popular, but she was from Hopkinton, a totally different clique.

Right around Halloween, Birdy Alves disappeared. For weeks the whole state was looking for her. Every night we'd see her face on the Providence news. If you have any information, they said, please call the Hopkinton police.

I loved my sister. I didn't want to believe she'd lie to me. Even now I want to believe she was trying to tell the truth that night our mother went out with Russ the firefighter, to warn me not to be like her. She might have. Nothing had happened yet. Later the police would put dates to everything, but for now we were two girls alone in a house on a Friday night with nowhere to go. We made popcorn and snuggled under an afghan on the couch with the lights out and watched *Mystic Pizza*, one of my mother's favorites, trading the bowl back and forth, our feet in each other's laps. She was Julia Roberts, I was Lili Taylor. It didn't matter that half the time she was on her phone. We didn't have to speak. All I wanted was to be close to her like this, the two of us laughing at the same places. She was the only one who knew what we'd both been through, and I liked to think we were inseparable, bound by more than just blood. We weren't happy that fall, in that rotting, underwater house, with everything we'd already lost, and everything still to come, but lying safe and warm under my grandmother's afghan, eating popcorn and stealing glances at my funny, beautiful sister as the light played over her face, I wished we could stay there forever.

1

Saturday Birdy's supposed to work her regular shift, ten to six, or so she's told everyone. Coming out of her mouth, it sounds like an alibi, the times too precise, when there's no need. Everyone knows her schedule.

Last night she couldn't sleep, and the light in the bathroom's too bright. In the mirror, the lacy red bra she's saved for today looks cheap, like she's trying too hard. She buttons her ugly uniform over it, ties her hair back, ducking her chin, trying not to meet her eyes. They're bloodshot and watery, not how she wants to look for him, and now she's caught, unable to look away.

What kind of person is she? Doesn't just asking that mean she has a conscience? She can't answer, lets the question pass. She's not going to stop anyway, so what's the point? Everything's wrong. It's cold and supposed to rain, canceling her daydreams of walking hand in hand with him on the beach, spreading a blanket in the dunes and lying down beside him to watch the clouds sail by. Behind her, sprawled on the bath mat, their cocker Ofelia watches her brush her teeth and rub lotion into her hands, stands before she's finished and points at the door, wagging her stubby tail like Birdy might take her with her.

"Stop. I can't open it when you're in my way." She understands she's being mean, but that only makes her more impatient. Ofelia knows her work clothes.

In her room she slips her makeup bag into her purse and sees she has one piece of gum left.

It's a bad idea, the whole thing. She's always thought of herself as honest, not perfect but good at heart, and the ease with which she's become this new, reckless Birdy is confusing, as if someone or something else has taken control of her. It's a kind of possession, a power greater than herself that at once exalts and leaves her helpless. It's not worth losing Hector over, yet here she is, already lost herself. Sometimes she doesn't care. Sometimes she wants to be nothing. The desire scares her, like her desire for Myles, at once baffling and all-consuming.

Downstairs her mother is sewing baby clothes for Birdy's new niece Luz in the Florida room, singing an old fado to herself like her grandmother used to. *My friend, I hate to leave you.* The machine chatters, stops, chatters again. If she could just sneak out without having to face her mother, she thinks, but the stairs, the door, the whole house creaks. Ofelia bounds down ahead of her, giving her away, the traitor. Before descending each step, Birdy has to think, like she's forgotten how to walk.

The machine chatters as she pulls on her puffy coat. She could go, just make a break for it, but she stands with her keys in hand, waiting for the needle to stop.

"I'm leaving," she calls.

With a scraping her mother gets up from her chair and comes to see her off, tottering on her bad knees, the good water glasses inside the hutch tinkling as she crosses the dining room. Her mother is the wisest person she knows, attuned to the whole family's moods. She knew Josefina was pregnant with Luz before Josefina did. Now Birdy's sure she can tell, and hugs her too tightly, makes a show of taking her stupid visor from its peg. Everything she does is a lie.

"We're having meatballs for supper. I figured I'd use up that hamburger before it goes bad."

"Good idea."

"Can you grab some Parmesan on your way home?"

"Sure," she says, knowing she'll never remember. She'll have to set a reminder on her phone.

Outside, the sky's brighter than she expected, light trying to break through the clouds. In the car it's a relief to slide on her sunglasses, like they might hide her, but there she is in the mirror, eyeless, alien. She might be an assassin from the future, coolly carrying out her mission, except she can't stop her thoughts. On the radio, the DJ makes a joke about the rain, talking over the opening of Rihanna's "Umbrella," and she turns it off. When

Myles had texted her, asking what she was doing Saturday, she threw her hands up and danced around her room like she'd won something. Now she has to remind herself that people do this all the time. She's not special.

She drives like she's going to work, down through Ashaway, where Hector's already punched in at the Liquor Depot. It's twenty-five miles an hour here, a speed trap to catch beach traffic coming off of 95. She doesn't want to get stopped, and slows as she passes the lot, hoping he'll see her go by, proof of her innocence. She searches for his Charger with its expensive rims—parked safely at the far end where no one can scratch the paint. When they first started dating, he'd come visit her at lunchtime, giving her his order, until she told him she didn't like it.

"What? I think you look cute in your uniform."

"I do not look cute, so don't, okay? I'm not joking."

"Okay," he said, disappointed, as if she were spoiling his fun. Lately Hector makes her feel as if she's being stingy, fending him off when he wants to hold her closer. He loves her, he says. He wants to marry her someday, have a houseful of babies like Kelvim and Josefina. He always wants something she's unwilling to give. How can she explain that she barely thinks of him? He never listens anyway. Myles asks her to tell stories about herself and hears every word.

Beyond the village post office, the speed limit changes back to forty, the oil-black river flashing through the trees, foaming over low dams. She's passed the long mill and the granite works with its uncut headstones a thousand times, so why do they call to her today? It's not just her mood, it's a spooky time of year.

The leaves are turning, Halloween's not that far off. They've already decorated at work, the front window hung with gauzy cotton spiderwebs. She imagines herself there, prepping for lunch, the doors locked, her biggest worry Sandra jamming the slicer.

She told Mr. Futterman she had a wedding to go to, making up a cousin. She knew he'd be fine with it. She never asks for Saturdays off, and the day shift is easy to cover.

Normally she'd take 3 all the way into Westerly. Now, before signaling for the turn onto the bypass, she checks her mirrors as if she's being followed—only a Roto-Rooter van that shoots past as she slows and takes the on-ramp. The bypass is a single lane each way, separated by a Jersey wall. Even in the off-season there's a steady line of traffic. She merges and settles in behind a pickup, just as the first drops of rain dot the windshield.

"You couldn't wait, could you?" She pulls off her sunglasses, folds them with one hand and drops them into the cupholder with her phone. A sprinkle at first, the rain gradually accelerates, tapping the glass, and by the time she reaches the light at the Post Road she has her wipers on high.

Again, the day is ruined, every sign arrayed against them. She can still end this, curl through the lot of the Stop & Shop and head back, swing by Elena's and confess before she does anything stupid, the two of them laughing at her Mission: Impossible trip. Chica, what are you thinking? I mean, Myles Parrish, boy is fine—I'm sorry, Hector—but what in the actual fuck are you thinking?

I don't know, Birdy thinks, but it's a lie. Anyone can see how her plan is going to turn out. She just doesn't want to take responsibility for it, as if she has no choice.

The light changes and she goes straight, past the entrance of the CVS and the Stop & Shop. Beside her, unbroken for a mile, runs the fence of the airport where the planes that tow the advertising banners for Foxwoods and Narragansett and the Wilcox Tavern take off. During the summer she's sat here in traffic with carloads of friends, and knows every restroom. Originally she'd weighed changing at the 99 Restaurant but worried that someone might see her. It's safer to do it farther down, at the park with the tennis courts, where she can lock the door.

With the rain, she's the only one there. The concrete floor is muddy with footprints and there's nowhere to hang her coat. She uses the knob, securing the collar with the straps of her purse. The air's dank, and when she pulls off her uniform tunic, a shiver ripples through her, raising goosebumps. She yanks on the top she's brought—a form-fitting ribbed red velour he likes—plucking at the shoulders in the mirror to get it to sit right. The fluorescent lighting is flat, and she leans across the sink to redo her eyeliner and brush on lip gloss, then stands back to appraise the transformation. This week she's second-guessed every choice of hers, and she's relieved to see there was no need. She's tempted to take a selfie—before and after—but just rolls up her tunic and shoves it in her purse, hauls her coat on and gets going, afraid of being late.

Back in the car she pops her last stick of gum and chews, her mouth filling with a sweet juice. She's close now. The road is so familiar, yet everything looks strange—giant boulders and dead rhododendrons on both sides, broken lobster traps for mailboxes.

A decommissioned buoy sits rusting in someone's front yard, the bottom dented like an old pot. She crests the final hill and there's the sea in the distance, a dark line. Far offshore, a ray of sunshine slants from a gap in the clouds, bronzing the water, picking out a tiny fishing boat. As she approaches the light at Shore Road, on cue it drops to green and she coasts through. After how much it's cost her to get here, it feels too easy.

The last half mile the land is absolutely flat, meadows edged with fallen stone walls, ponds and marshlands ringed with shaggy reeds. The pastel motels and gray-shingled guest cottages are closed, their driveways roped off. NO TURNAROUNDS, a sign anchored by a whitewashed concrete block says, as if she still could. The sidewalks are empty, only a few puffed-up gulls perched on pilings, the wind ruffling their feathers. Ahead, where the road T-bones Atlantic Avenue, a police SUV cruises through the intersection, startling her. She waits an extra second at the stop sign before turning the other way, passing a nostalgic four-sided clock showing the wrong time, and there in front of her, beyond the padlocked batting cages and go-kart track, spreads her destination, the vast asphalt parking lot of the state beach.

The lot's shaped like a racetrack, a giant oval with the entrance at the finish. On Governor's Bay Day, when admission's free, she and her friends have waited hours to file through the tollbooths, inching along the guardrail, so close, sometimes getting turned away, paying extra to park in people's yards. Today there's no line. As she follows the road around, she's surprised to see anyone, but there are always diehards. In the near corner, just past the last ramshackle beach bar, two

RVs huddle against the dunes, then for a long stretch there's nothing but puddles, rafts of gulls driven inland, all facing the same way. Through the breaks in the dunes she can see waves crashing, throwing up foam. Farther down the lot, this side of the bathhouse, there's a clot of cars. Even from a distance she can tell most of them are trucks—and he'd be by himself, not with a bunch of other people.

He's not here, Birdy thinks. Somehow the girlfriend has found out—the girlfriend whose name she hates, flinching when she hears it on TV, or worse, in church; the girlfriend she pretends not to imagine him with every weekend, at movies and parties, making out on couches, wearing earrings he's given her. She doesn't care where they go or what they do, as if his life apart from Birdy doesn't matter. When Birdy thinks of her, a saving blankness overcomes her. Even now Birdy's face is changing, pinched with the effort of erasing her. Birdy doesn't want to take her place, Birdy wants her to have never existed. The idea that she's had Myles to herself for three years is paralyzing, a mistake Birdy likes to think he's too nice to fix. She'd hoped today was going to be a big step for both of them, so why, turning in at the tollbooths, as she spies his Eclipse alone on the far side of the bathhouse, does her stomach drop?

Is she late? How long has he been waiting for her?

It's all she's wanted, to be with him, but now it feels criminal, like a drug deal. Cutting across the empty spaces, she fumbles with her phone, holding down the button to turn it off, the screen finally going black. She spits her gum into a tissue, shoves the wad in the ashtray, getting rid of the evidence.

As she pulls up beside him, he steps out, popping open an umbrella, and comes around to shield her from the rain, just like in the song. He offers his hand as if asking her to dance. She takes it and steps out into the wind and cold, the ocean thundering beyond the dunes, and before she can say a word, he kisses her, his mouth hot, his body hard against hers, and she forgets everything else. They're totally exposed, their cars, their license plates. Somewhere someone's watching them on surveillance cameras, but she doesn't care.

"I missed you," he says.

"I missed *you*," she says, and kisses him again, greedily, like the first wasn't enough.

"Come on." He opens the door for her and she ducks in, the warmth and the scent of his cherry vanilla air freshener enveloping her. She watches him circle the hood, then, as if they've been married for years, reaches across the driver's seat for the handle and opens his door for him.

Again they kiss—across the emergency brake, twisted, straining to meet each other. His hands are cold and her coat's in the way. She wants to pull it off, but it's awkward, the space is too cramped, and without having to speak, agreeing it's impossible, they part and subside, beaming, drinking each other in, amazed that they're really here, that after all the arduous hours apart they've found each other again. Somehow it's funny, how easy it is when they're together. The rest of the world disappears, and everything's right again. He clips in his seatbelt and waits for her to do the same, wheels the car around and guns it for the exit.

"Where are we going?" she asks, teasing.

He gives her a smile as if she's said the right thing. "You'll see."

It's a busy day, even with the rain. Saturdays are always crazy, and now with the weather, people have nothing to do but shop. They come in soaked, their hair matted down, yellow slickers and umbrellas dripping on the carpet. Normally Angel wouldn't mind. She likes the rain and how dark it is while she's warm and dry inside. Plus when it's busy, the day goes faster. She and Shayna don't have to straighten shelves or police the lot, where friends driving by might see them. They hang behind the registers, bantering, singing along with the piped-in music when it's good, goofing on it when it's bad. Beyoncé's "Single Ladies" is on heavy rotation, and Shayna's been trying to teach her the moves from the video. Angel's more into Paramore and Fall Out Boy, but the chorus is irresistible. *If you liked it then you shoulda put a ring on it.*

The problem is, everyone's using coupons to stock up on Halloween candy, and one of the prices in the weekly flyer is wrong. All afternoon people have been arguing with her over fun-size Snickers bars, waving the ad in her face as if she's lying to them. It's like Shayna says: Never forget the customer is your enemy.

"We're sorry for the misprint," Mr. Fenton tells them to say.

"I'm sorry you're so cheap," Angel wants to tell the customers, just to shut them up. It's not even a dollar, and they're already getting a dollar off with the coupon. What do they want?

"I want to talk to the manager," they say, letting her know she's beneath them, and she has to call him to the front, where he tells them the exact same thing, except they don't talk to him like he's a child, because he has a penis.

"The shelf has the right price on it," Shayna complains.

"What we need to do," Angel says, so Mr. Fenton can hear her, "is get rid of the flyers. That's what we need to do."

"Too late. They went out Tuesday."

"I mean the ones by the door. No one's bringing them from home." Which is not exactly true. She's seen a couple folded small with the item circled in thick Sharpie like it's a kind of treasure. These are the same people who clear the shelves of Dove bodywash when there's a rebate. They probably have closets full of it, whole garages.

Mr. Fenton can't even pull the flyers without calling someone, but it's the weekend, and while he's in back, another customer around her mother's age ducks in out of the rain and heads for the seasonal aisle.

"Sweet, sweet candy," Shayna says.

"This is stupid," Angel says, and crosses the darkened carpet, grabs the whole stack and shoves it under the counter.

"I think he'll notice."

"I don't care."

"How about if I just cut that part out?"

"No," Angel says. "It's not *your* fault it's wrong."

Of course, the woman's buying three bags of Snickers. Angel advises her of the price before bothering to scan them.

"That's not what it says here." Close up, she's older than her mother, and smaller, her hair hennaed, her eyebrows dyed black. Her glasses are on a bead chain, like a librarian's.

"I know, it's a misprint. We're very sorry. Do you still want to buy them?"

"The only reason I drove all the way here in the rain was to get these, and you won't honor the price you've advertised?"

"It was a misprint. We're very sorry."

"What about the other prices in here? Are they wrong too?"

"As far as we know, just that one."

"Well, that's convenient."

"You know there's a coupon for them in the paper, a dollar off."

"That doesn't help me, does it?"

The woman's part betrays her gray roots. Angel is a good foot taller than her, and strong from weight training for volleyball and breaking down boxes every day. Even with the counter between them, she could easily reach across and grab the chain of the woman's glasses, twist it and pull her close, all the while looking into her eyes. Maybe she'd change her tone then.

Angel smiles. "Let me see if I can dig one up for you."

The zippered bank pouch under the register is stuffed with them, and she plucks one out and scans the barcode—peep, peep, peep. "How's that? That'll be six twenty-seven. Do you have an ExtraCare card?"

The woman hesitates like it's a trick, then pulls her card out of her wallet. How easily people are pacified. "You still need to fix the price."

"We're working on it," Angel says, folding the receipt into the bag and offering it to her by the handles. "Thank you. Take care now."

"I saw what you did there," Shayna says when they're alone again.

"I know, one per customer. I was getting ready to lose my shit."

"I thought for sure you were going to go off on her."

"It's not worth it."

The store phone rings, and before Angel can react, Shayna touches her finger to her nose.

It's Mr. Fenton, and Angel thinks she's in trouble. From his office, he can see them on the store's security cams. It's one of their running jokes, how he watches them like porn. If they installed a paywall, they could be making so much money.

"Please go through the flyers and take that page out. If they ask specifically, then go ahead and give them the price."

"The wrong price," Angel says.

"That is correct."

"Okay," she says, as if it's crazy, and tells Shayna.

"Like I said," Shayna says.

"Jesus, make up your mind, right?"

They leaf through the flyers one at a time, sliding out the page and folding them again, replacing the stack in the rack by the door. It takes maybe five minutes, so why does it bother her?

It's not the job or the day. Lately she feels impatient with everything, even when things go right. They're seniors. Next year Shayna and Myles and all her friends on the volleyball team will be off at college, and Angel will still be stuck in Ashaway with Marie and her mother, working days and going to CCRI part-time. Myles was her first, Myles is her only. She knows she'll lose him to some rich girl, and there's nothing she can do. Lately at night she can't sleep, hounded by the idea, powerless, switching pillows, listening to her heart beat in her ears, and wonders if this is why people kill themselves.

"I hate my life," she tells Shayna, deadpan, the two of them standing like mannequins at their registers.

"I hate your life too," Shayna says. "You can go on break if you want."

Smoking in the cold on the loading dock, she texts Myles: *MU.* They're supposed to see *Zombieland* tonight, which sounds stupid to her, but there's nothing else playing. After, they'll meet up with everyone at Ryan Dineen's, and Myles will play a few of his songs while they sit around the bonfire, dipping his head, his voice low with sorrow, and Angel will watch the other girls watching his fingers spider over the strings, falling for him the same way she did. She'd rather be alone with him. They could go to the beach if the rain stops, make their own fire.

Bch l8r? she adds and hits send.

She watches the screen like he'll reply immediately. Normally he's good at getting back to her, but he's working, and after a while she gives up and finishes her cigarette, looking out at the traffic swishing past, still hoping her phone might ding. Before going in, she checks again, frowning, and sees she still has three more hours. That's the problem with having a phone, she thinks. You always know exactly what time it is.

★ ★ ★

She's never stolen anything, only a few dollars from her mother's purse. This is how it must feel, Birdy thinks, propped on a pillow in a strange bed, watching him come back from the bathroom naked, long and lean, and stop to rearrange the fire with a pair of wrought-iron tongs. The curtains are open, the picture window facing the waves. Anyone walking on the beach could see him if it wasn't raining—could see them, coupling unashamed, sprawled across the sheets, drinking champagne in the middle of the day. She's strolled past these summer homes her entire life, picking out her favorites with her friends. She never imagined actually being inside one, not like this.

The room isn't his. Beyond the nautical decor, he doesn't need a king bed and two dressers, and the night table on her side holds a collection of knickknacks, including a wooden sandpiper standing on one leg. What does it mean if this is his parents' bed? She'd like to believe she's the first girl he's brought here, even if it's not true. So much of love is pretending.

"More?" he asks, pointing to the bottle.

"Sure," she says, though it's already giving her a headache. She hasn't eaten all day, but it's too late to ask about lunch.

He climbs in beside her and raises his glass, pushes his hair away from his face like Keanu. "To us."

"To us," she says, and searches his eyes before taking a sip. For so long this is all she's wanted, so why does it terrify her? Now that she has him, she's afraid of losing him. She's afraid none of this is real.

"I'm cold," she says, so that he'll hold her. She pulls the sheet up over them, the two of them hiding in their own warm, white world.

His hands can't keep still. Unlike Hector, he waits for her to roll his way, the two of them face-to-face, entwined, gently rocking. How perfectly they fit. He's quiet, so she is too. She meets him, intent, matching his pace, spurring him with her hands and heels. He tenses, growling low in his throat, sinks back again.

They stay that way, nose-to-nose under the covers. He traces the gold pendant that spells out her name.

"Why do they call you Birdy?" They're so close he only has to whisper.

"My father called me that when I was little because I was always singing."

"You never told me you could sing."

"I can't."

"Sing something for me."

"I can't sing like you can."

"Sing something you'd sing when you were little."

She puts her mouth to his ear and coos: *Soy Oquendo, soy Oquendo, madre si a fi attendo.*

"What does it mean?"

"It doesn't mean anything, it's just a rhyme I made up."

"It's pretty." He sings it back to her, deeper, too serious, as if he's making fun of her.

"Stop."

"I like it."

"Shhh," she says, and for a while he's quiet.

"Let me get rid of this," he says, and slides out to go to the bathroom.

In the grate the fire crackles. The rain streaks the window. Outside, the waves break and fall, tireless, lulling. She's drowsy from the champagne and being up most of the night, and when he comes back they lie together in silence, sated, his arm a pleasant weight as she slips from one dream into another.

The plane to Block Island wakes them, droning over the house, flying low across the water. The room's dark, the fire embers. For a moment Birdy thinks she's late, that her mother will be calling to see where she is, but it's not even five-thirty, the sun's just going down.

"When do you have to be back?" Myles asks, like he doesn't have any plans, when she knows there's a party at Ryan's. For a moment she sees what a mistake this is.

They take a shower together, a precaution she hadn't thought of, but their bodies are so warm and fresh after that they end up making love on the rug by the fireplace. The day's over, the champagne's killed. It's time to go. She has to find her clothes, scattered around the room like an explosion. In the mirror, impossibly, she looks the same. He makes the bed and sits on the edge, grinning, watching her finish getting dressed. She stands over him, cradles his head against her chest as if he might hear her heart beating and know what she's feeling.

"When am I going to see you again?" she asks, and she can feel him stiffen. Even to her it sounds like an ultimatum.

"What are you doing Wednesday?"

"Working."

"I'm working Tuesday and Thursday."

They don't bother trying Friday and Saturday night, like they're off-limits. She shouldn't have said anything. She shouldn't even be here.

"What are you doing Sunday?" he asks.

Sunday's eight days away. "I knew this would happen. I'm so stupid."

"Stop. No you're not." He pulls her closer. "What are you doing tomorrow?"

Tomorrow. How eagerly she seizes this gift—no matter what she has to do—as proof they want the same thing. She clings to the promise as she follows him downstairs, turning off the lights as they go, locking up. He's parked his car in the garage, and before he can thumb the button for the overhead door, she kisses him to apologize for ruining the mood. How can she explain that she doesn't know what she's doing?

"What was that for?" he asks.

"Nothing."

It's like night out, and still raining, long drops knifing through their headlights, the great salt pond to their right a void. Between the heater and the air freshener, the interior's stifling. He shifts up and rests his hand on her thigh, and she covers it. They could be headed out to dinner, the evening just beginning. She should be ashamed, yet instead of guilty she feels proud, as if, together, they've accomplished something impossible. Splashing along in the dark, leaving the house behind, she already misses the fireplace and the view from the room. If she never sees them again, at least for a few hours she knew them.

"I like hearing you sing," he says.

Does he know what he does to her? How is she supposed to go back and pretend she just went to work?

"Tomorrow you can sing to me," she says.

"That's fair." Another promise to hold on to.

Ahead, backlit, the black bulk of the old carousel pavilion looms out of the darkness. They pass the RV park and the Water Wizz and the mini golf, closed for the season, and there across the lot is the bathhouse, and her car, all by itself. Myles slows and turns in at the tollbooths.

She only means to kiss him goodbye but they don't know how to stop. They clutch at each other like fighters. A reckless part of her wants him to leave strawberries on her neck.

"It's not fair," she says playfully.

"I know. I'll text you later."

A final kiss, and another, stolen. "Stop."

"You stop."

"Go."

"I'm going."

He doesn't get out with the umbrella, something she mulls as she starts the car. At least he waits for her. At the tollbooths they go their separate ways. She honks, he honks back. In the mirror his taillights grow smaller and smaller, then vanish around the curve so there's only night behind her.

She stops at the stop sign, though there's no cop in sight. The old clock is still wrong. After being so close, it's strangely freeing to be alone, her mind emptying, finally at rest.

"Myles, Myles, Myles, Myles," she says, as if casting a spell. Inside her, the tiniest seed opens. She knows she shouldn't hope. She's already done everything she said she wouldn't do, so why stop now?

At the tennis courts she doesn't bother going into the bathroom, just unbuckles her seat belt and pulls her shirt over her head. It's cold and the shirt smells like smoke. She didn't wash her hair, and wonders if it does too. Buttoning up her uniform in the shadows, she thinks she should be glad she's not good at this, but it only makes her feel worse, as if she's already been caught.

Before she gets going, she can't resist turning on her phone—another mistake. She expects a voicemail from Hector, questions that will force her to come up with an explanation, but there's nothing except a reminder to buy Parmesan cheese.

She has the time, the Stop & Shop's right up the road, so why does it make her feel tired?

The store's too bright and busy, people like her grabbing last-minute ingredients for dinner. The crowd and the wait at the express lane strip the day of whatever romance it had, and now she worries about tomorrow, whether Myles only offered because she pushed him. That's not what they wanted this to be. She wants to text him and say it's okay if they don't see each other tomorrow, but it's not true—it's all she wants.

"Hey Birdy, nice outfit." Three people behind her stands Mikayla in her PetSmart top with an armful of tortilla chips.

"Hey, Mikayla." They're not really friends, they're just in the same PE class and study hall. She's nice enough but has always seemed to Birdy like the girlfriend, big and blonde with perfect teeth, very vanilla.

"You going to Ryan's later?"

"Not if it's raining like this."

"I hear you."

The cashier is someone's grandmother and can't get things to scan. Finally it's Birdy's turn. She pays cash and doesn't need a bag.

"Maybe see you later," Mikayla says.

"Maybe."

She flees into the night with her cheese, almost dropping it as she tries to open the car one-handed. If this is how it's going to be, she doesn't think she can do it. And this is just the first time.

Back on the road, anonymous again, she shakes her head at the close call, rolls her eyes, laughing at herself. Why would anyone ever be afraid of nice, white-bread Mikayla? And Mikayla seeing her actually fits her alibi. Everything's fine, and when she slows for the speed trap in Ashaway and the Liquor Depot, Hector's Charger is gone, as it should be. The speed limit switches and she hits the gas, keeping pace with the long line headed for 95. She's remembered the cheese and she'll be home right on time. For now, at least, she's getting away with it.

Carol should be punched out by now, headed home to get ready for her date, but Mrs. Landrum is dehydrated and won't eat, and she can't leave until they've calmed her down. It's been happening more often lately, even on the soft diet. After a spoon or two of broth she starts spluttering, grabbing at her throat with both hands like someone's choking her. Jell-O, oatmeal, pureed squash—everything triggers her gag reflex. The nutritionist says it has nothing to do with the food. The muscles of the esophagus weaken. It's about positioning. She needs to sit up and tuck her chin, make that pipe nice and straight—hard to do when she's even more disoriented than normal.

For the dehydration, they use a saline solution, which she resists because the needle leaves huge blooming bruises that are sore for days. She cries like a child when she sees Carol fixing the drip.

"I'm sorry, hon," Carol says, turning her wrist over. "I promise I'll be quick."

She'll be the villain. She's used to it, and fair or not, she doesn't trust anyone on nights. Just look at that abscess. It's a miracle the family hasn't sued them.

"Hold my hand, dear. Tighter. That's it."

Her skin is like rice paper, nearly see-through. There's no need to bear down—that's the mistake the younger nurses make, sticking it in too deep, breaking through layers of tissue. The trick is to go in shallow, slip it into the vein as if fishing out a splinter.

"All done," Carol says, squeezing her shoulder, but Mrs. Landrum won't be consoled.

"Why are you hurting me?" she pleads.

In some dire cases, Carol can't come up with an honest answer, but Mrs. Landrum isn't one of them. She still has years of skilled care to go. "You need to rehydrate. This is going to help you do that."

"Where's my daughter? I want my daughter."

"I know, hon. I'm here with you. I'm going to make sure you get something to eat."

Pumping the foot pedal to raise the bed, she checks her watch. Russ is picking her up at seven. She hopes there's a pizza left in the freezer, otherwise she has nothing for the girls for dinner.

Mrs. Landrum is staring into space, and Carol waves a hand to bring her back. "How we doing there, Vera? Want to try some creamed spinach?"

"I'll try."

"How's that? Is that better?"

Mrs. Landrum nods, swallowing.

"There you go." She eats so slowly, every bite a production. Carol's already late but sits by her side, feeding her spoonful by spoonful like a child.

Who will do this for her? No one, Carol thinks. Unlike Aunt Mil, who lives on the second floor, she could never afford the Elms. Mrs. Landrum's a millionaire. Her husband owned a paint factory in Stonington that's still in business. On her wall hangs a picture of him at the helm of a yacht, wearing an admiral's cap and smoking a pipe. Carol's lived here her whole life and only been on a boat like that once, temping at a wedding in Watch Hill. They motored out around Napatree Point near sunset and came back to the lights of the yacht club glittering on the water. Even after passing hors d'oeuvres all night she had to admit it was magical.

The drip's half empty by the time Mrs. Landrum finishes her tray.

"I guess I was hungry," Mrs. Landrum says.

"I guess so," Carol says, and cleans her up, gets her settled again. Her hope, which goes against twenty years of experience, is that if she treats every resident this way, maybe people will take the same care with Aunt Mil. But even she has to pray for patience sometimes.

Driving home in a drizzle, she thinks the world is unfair. She doesn't want her girls to have to take care of her. She wants them to get out of Ashaway and have families of their own, but exactly how that will happen she can't imagine. Angel has her looks but her temper too. Marie's bright but afraid of everything, which Carol thinks is partly her fault and partly Frank's. The plan for now is to get them through high school and help them as much as they can with college, which in her case seems more and more impossible, unless something big changes. As someone whose dreams didn't work out, she sees the future as beyond her control, random, their lives at the mercy of chance, even if they do everything right.

There is a pizza, so she doesn't have to spend money ordering one. Angel's going out and has left the bathroom a mess, which starts an argument Carol doesn't have time for. "This whole house is a mess," she shouts from the landing, "because no one cleans anything around here except me." It's her job—Mom the bulldozer, Mom the bitch.

Upstairs, she closes her door and strips off her scrubs. The dress she wanted to wear is too tight around her middle, and she tosses it on the bed and tries another before settling on an old favorite, basic black with a scooped neck. It's their second date, and after the first, at Ella's, she suspects he's taking her somewhere nice. Cocktails, a bottle of wine with dinner, maybe a nightcap at his place, which she's yet to see. After a day like today, she needs a night out.

Neither of the girls says anything about her dress or her earrings. They've seen it all before.

By itself, the pizza doesn't seem enough, but there are no salad makings, just some old coleslaw, and she apologizes for the crappy dinner.

"I like pizza," Marie says, ever agreeable, which only makes her feel worse.

"It doesn't matter to me," Angel says, messing with her phone, ignoring the TV. "I'm going out."

"You need to eat something."

"I will."

"Can you help me with this?" Carol asks Marie, handing over her necklace and lifting her hair in back so she can do the clasp. "Thank you. How do I look?"

"Ravishing," Marie says, a line stolen from an old movie.

"So, this is your third date?" Angel asks.

"Second."

"You're not counting the first."

"Don't be smart."

"For a third date, it looks about right."

"What does that mean?"

"It means you're looking good but you're not trying too hard."

"Thank you, I think."

"You look nice, Mom," Marie says.

"Thank you, Mimi. Tomorrow after church I'm going big food shopping, so if there's anything anyone wants, put it on the list."

Her peace offering produces a rare truce, and for a few minutes, waiting for the oven timer to ding, the three of them are all there together, a state even more precious because it can't last. Carol pours herself a glass of wine and stands behind the couch, admiring her girls, who deserve so much more than she can give them. She can still rest a hand on Marie's shoulder and she won't pull away. Her baby, already thirteen—but a young thirteen, not like Carol when she was her age, smoking weed and meeting boys at the pond below the cemetery. She used to worry that Angel would be wild like her. This generation's tame, raised on D.A.R.E. programs and designated drivers. Even in her twenties, Carol was never that responsible. Even now she still gets high once in a while, drinks too much, sleeps with the wrong guy, and if she regrets any of it, that's her business, no one else's. She wants better for her girls.

Outside, a car pulls into the drive, headlights sweeping over the front windows. The pizza dings, then Angel's phone, making Carol do a double take. It's Myles in his tricked-out Eclipse. He reminds Carol of Frank when he was his age, lanky and slim-hipped, bombing around in a jacked-up Camaro, looking for the next good time. Though they've been together forever, Carol doesn't trust him. That he's from money makes it harder for her to believe he's serious. She worries that Angel is making the same mistake she did. She didn't listen to her mother either.

"What time will you be home?"

"Late."

"Not too late. Text me if you're going to be later than midnight."

"I'm going to be later than midnight."

"Then text me."

"I will."

"Be careful, sweetie."

"You too," Angel says, getting the last word, and closes the front door.

Carol pulls the pizza out and lets it cool a few minutes. On the couch, Marie is watching some nature documentary about wildebeests fording a river, an afghan thrown over her legs like an old lady. She's been home by herself all day, and Carol feels bad that she's leaving again. She'd suggest going over to her mother's place for the evening but is afraid Marie might take it the wrong way. She doesn't need a babysitter.

"You gonna be okay here?"

"Yeah," Marie says, lukewarm. "What time will you be home?"

"Not too late. Don't wait up for me though." Because she will. Carol will find her passed out under the afghan with the TV on and have to guide her upstairs like a sleepwalker. In the morning, Marie won't remember anything, only that she never came home.

Russ is right on time, parking and ringing the doorbell like a normal person, waving to Marie from the front hall as if he's never set foot in the house before. Carol's intuition is right. He's wearing a jacket and tie, and she needles him for not telling her they were going somewhere fancy. She grabs her good dress coat, her keys and her purse and kisses Marie goodbye, making sure the door is locked behind her.

She doesn't recognize the car Russ is driving, a huge black Cadillac SUV he has to help her climb into using the lighted running board, not easy in heels. The leather smells new. With his suit and tie, she wonders if in his off-hours he's a limo driver, the ride a perk.

"Fancy schmancy."

"I figured it was more appropriate for where we're going."

"And where would that be?"

"That would be Ledyard." Meaning the casino.

"I'm not a big gambler," she says, hoping he won't be disappointed.

"I'm not either, I just like to eat. There's a new steak place from the guy on *Top Chef* that just opened."

She follows the show and imagines Russ at home, watching it by himself, like Marie and her wildebeests. He's divorced, so maybe he watched it with his ex. Like the car, it's a mystery. How little she knows him, yet she feels safe, maybe because he's older, and considerate, and smart. After the last few idiots, she's thinks it's a good sign that he's not her type.

At the casino, he skips the parking lots and glides right up to the main entrance, leaves the car running for the valet while he helps her down. She takes his arm, and the doors part for them. Inside it's bright and busy as a mall, the air tropical, a waterfall dropping three stories into a pool full of fat koi. The floors are marble, the chrome and glass concourse they funnel through lined with designer shops aimed at high rollers: Versace, Burberry, Prada. Though the restaurant just opened, Russ seems to know where he's going, taking a shortcut through a carpeted parlor of jangling slot machines, a right by the blinking marquee of the arena where the WNBA team plays, then a left into a dead end, and there it is, Craft, absolutely packed, spillover milling outside in groups, everyone dressed for the evening.

Russ heads directly for the stand. The maître d' has their reservation and hands them off to a greeter built like a ballerina who leads them past the clatter and leaping flames of the open kitchen and through the noisy main room to a secluded booth in the far corner. The place is all blond wood and black leather, the wineglasses on the table oversized and fragile-looking.

The menu the aproned server presents her doesn't have any prices. When he leaves, she turns it to show Russ.

"It's all free," he says, spreading his hands wide, and when she reaches to see his, he pulls it back. "My choice, my treat."

"Okay," she says, unconvinced. "Next time I choose where we go."

"That's fair."

They order the fancy house cocktails without names—Tequila for her, Bourbon for him—but she can't let it go. She leans closer so no one will hear. "Like, how expensive? What's the most expensive thing?"

"You don't want to know."

"I do."

"The wagyu ribeye for two."

"How much is it?"

"Are you ready?"

She nods, steeling herself to hear a hundred, a hundred twenty-five.

"Market price."

"You're a jerk."

He covers the other prices to show her—MP.

"You're still a jerk."

"Want to order it? I'll split it with you."

"No. I'm not a big ribeye person. I'd rather have a filet."

"I'm with you," he says. "The filet's a perfect steak."

Her cocktail has pineapple juice and jalapeño and a sprig of rosemary, and is gone by the time the bread arrives. They order a second round, and then a bottle of red the server pours into a beakerlike decanter. Russ raises his glass to her, and they clink—"*Salut.*" From the first sip she can tell it's better than anything she buys.

Her filet arrives on a wooden plank, bloody, already sliced, a presentation she's never seen before. Along with sautéed button mushrooms and blue cheese crumbles, Russ has ordered a side of creamed spinach for them, making her picture Mrs. Landrum, but it's rich and salty, easily the best she's ever had. She tries not to think of Marie and her pizza, of Angel and Myles riding around town.

The server refills her glass, tipping out the last drops.

"Do we want another bottle?" Russ asks, like it's up to her.

She can see which way he's leaning, his eyes merry, and the evening's been so nice. She may regret it tomorrow, but for now, eating her perfect steak, surrounded by the buzzing room full of beautiful strangers, she's happy, free, for a few hours, of everyone who needs her.

"Yes," she says. "We do."

Marie knows she shouldn't eat the whole pizza, but it's hard when there's nothing else to do and it's sitting right behind her on the cutting board, still warm. It's a staple, along with frozen fried chicken and Swanson potpies, a quick and easy dinner her mother can throw in the oven when she gets home. Normally Marie splits one with her mother or Angel, whoever doesn't have a date, but some nights, like tonight, they both go out, and she has to eat alone. It's a trap. Tomorrow her mother will ask if there were any leftovers, making her say it, when all she has to do is look in the fridge. At the least Marie needs to leave two pieces, which sounds easy except she's watching TV and every other commercial is for fast food—McDonald's, Taco Bell, until finally, like a sign, an ad runs for Pizza Hut's stuffed-crust pizza—*No one OutPizzas the Hut*—sending her into the kitchen with her plate.

She leaves the two smallest pieces, pulling a loose pepperoni from one edge, and resettles herself on the couch. She's a fast eater, her mother's always telling her to slow down, but there's no one here to watch her now. With both hands she folds the slice into a V, raises it to her lips and feeds it into her mouth like a log into a buzz saw, gobbling bite after greasy bite until her cheeks are filled and she has to breathe through her nose to chew. The pizza itself is crappy, it's this feeling she loves, of being overwhelmed, drowning in sensation, the way she feels when she touches herself in the shower—followed by the same shame, the same promises to change and the inevitable guilt when she gives in again. It's a kind of high she knows is wrong but can't stop wanting.

She's just shoved the second slice in her mouth when someone pulls up outside. Busted, she thinks it's her mother and Russ. She jumps up to ditch her plate in the sink, trips over the afghan and almost chokes on the wad of dough, tears coming to her eyes. She spits the mouthful into the hole of the disposal, races back to the couch and pretends she's watching TV.

A key grates in the lock, the door swings open, and it's Angel, with Myles behind her, carrying a cardboard liquor box he tries to hide.

"Criminy, you scared me. I thought you were Mom."

"I forgot something," Angel says, stopping behind the couch to block her view while Myles heads upstairs.

"Oh yeah?" Marie says, making a show of watching him. "What?"

"None of your beeswax."

"More like boozewax."

"Funny not funny," Angel says, and heads up after him.

Marie hears her door close and peers at the ceiling as if she can see them crossing the floor to her bed. She knows what they do. She's seen porn. Angel's even shown her a dick pic someone sent to her phone as a prank, something she's never told her mother because she'd make a big deal of it. Once, at their last place, when her mother was out with Wes, Myles came over with his guitar and Angel told her to go watch TV in the other room. It's not something Marie likes to picture, the same way she doesn't like to imagine her mother with Russ, or anyone, even her father. The whole idea is strange. What do they say to each other when it's over?

It's only been a minute when the door opens and Myles comes down by himself. Marie's very aware that they're alone and concentrates on the TV. With his gray eyes and easy smile, he seems beautiful to her, a prince in disguise. An innocent, she thinks he doesn't know she has a crush on him.

"Marie the Bee who lives up in a tree, what you got for me?"

"Nothing."

"Hey, pizza," he says, grabbing a slice. "What else you got going on tonight?"

"Nothing."

"You are a fun one, I don't care what anybody says. Aren't there any scary movies on?"

"They scare me."

"That's good—they're supposed to give you endorphins." He crams the last bite of crust in his mouth and brushes his hands over the sink. "Have you seen *The Shining*? You've got to see *The Shining*."

"She doesn't need to see *The Shining*," Angel says, coming down the stairs. "She's all by herself in a creepy old house next to an abandoned mill in a shitty little town. She's already in a Stephen King movie."

"Zing," Myles says.

"Thanks," Marie says. "That's helpful."

"We weren't here," Angel says.

"Who said that?" Marie asks.

"Exactly."

"Watch *The Shining*!" Myles calls over his shoulder, and they're gone.

Peeking around the drapes, she watches them back out and take off down the road before she goes upstairs. There's no lock on Angel's door, or her closet. Like any kid sister, Marie is a sneak, and knows everyone's hiding places. Vibrators, love letters, weed, condoms—nothing's safe from her. The box is right where she figured it would be, in the far corner, tucked under a hanging storage bag, behind the milk crate that holds her roller skates, draped with an old electric blanket. It's heavy, which is why Myles was carrying it. Marie undoes the flaps, expecting to see bottles. Instead, what she finds is a pink tank of gas with a brass valve like the propane her father hooks up to their grill. The tank is unmarked, but the bag of balloons convinces her it's helium. With so little to go on, she can only deduce that they're throwing a surprise party for someone. The question is who. Her birthday isn't for months, or their mother's. Maybe a friend, or an anniversary. Maybe the tank is stolen.

Downstairs, she wraps the last piece of pizza in a generous sheet of aluminum foil, folding it like gift wrap, making the one piece look like two, arranging the package on the second shelf of the fridge where it's partially eclipsed by a gallon of milk and her mother's jug wine. She wipes off the cutting board, dumping the crumbs in the sink, and goes back to watching TV, where Jennifer Love Hewitt is solving a mystery in a tight sweater and pencil skirt.

It's unfair, Marie thinks. Even if she was going to kill the whole thing, the choice has been stolen from her, and she can't tell her mother or Angel will be pissed at her. She can't keep her mind on the plot of *Ghost Whisperer*, sits there protesting inwardly until a commercial comes on, throws off the afghan and goes into the kitchen. She takes the last piece from the fridge, unfolds the foil and sticks it in the toaster oven, then after a minute pulls it out—still cold—flops it on a plate and nukes it in the microwave. It comes out molten, the crust so wet she can't pick it up and has to use a knife and fork. The cheese burns the roof of her mouth, but she doesn't care. She shovels in bite after bite till it's all gone, snuffling as she chews and swallows, transported, for one fleeting moment, knowing she'll pay for it later.

As they cruise by Ryan Dineen's, Birdy searches the yard for his car. She should be relieved she doesn't see it—she'll see him tomorrow—but she's disappointed, as if he's stood her up. It wasn't her idea to come. All night she avoided mentioning the party, hoping Hector might forget it, and then after the movie, when they'd agreed on Friendly's, Gregory had to text him. She should have known. It's Westerly. There's nowhere else to go.

The whole school's here, cars lining both sides of the road. Hector takes a minute to find the perfect spot, doing a u-ey, pulling off well past everyone else, tucked up to a neighbor's driveway so they can't get blocked in. He always does this, but tonight it grates on her. She unbuckles her belt before he's done, and the warning pings.

"Hang on a second," he says, like he's in charge.

"Hanging."

The rain's finally stopped. She's surprised to find she misses it, the way she misses the afternoon, the waves breaking along the beach like white lace. The trees are dripping, the air's cold and smells of woodsmoke, a foretaste of winter. As they hike up the driveway in the weak glow of the coach light, Hector takes her hand as if to show everyone they're together, a habit she now wishes she hadn't encouraged. It's not his fault. Again, she wants to defend him against her newfound cruelty. He's not the one who's changed. Even in this she's selfish. She wants to believe what's happening has nothing to do with him.

It's a Halloween party, though Halloween's like a month away. Ghosts hang from the trees, and the yard's dotted with fake gravestones bearing names like Ima Goner and Yul B. Next. Dry-ice fog wafts from the porch, wall-to-wall with people in costume, Dracula and Spider-Man and Hermione grooving to the music booming inside, shivering the windows in their frames.

"Hey, Birdy." Mikayla is Britney Spears in pigtails and a girls' school uniform, dancing, waving around a Solo cup over her head.

"Hey, Mikayla," she says, wishing she had a disguise.

The keg's in back, and Hector leads her through the house. It's impossible to hear with the music, the bass thudding inside her chest. The furniture has been cleared out to make a dance floor, strobe lights flashing from the mantel, freezing the crowd in ecstatic poses. Normally she'd be on the floor, forcing Hector to join her, but with no chance of seeing Myles, the whole thing feels like a waste of time. They've just gotten here and already she wants to leave. She could be at home, asleep and dreaming of him. Instead, she has to pretend she's having fun.

Gregory and Sonya are hanging out in the kitchen, and they stop on the way through to say hey, Hector giving him a bro hug as if he hasn't just seen him all day at work. Sonya air-kisses her to save her makeup.

"Girlfriend, you are looking superfine," Sonya says, as if she can tell.

"Thanks. I like your nails," Birdy says, before Hector drags her away.

She's almost glad Elena's not there. She doesn't feel like seeing anyone, even her. Everyone's talking, talking, talking. What do they all have to talk about?

Hector pays her cover without asking, another debt she can't repay. She doesn't want to drink too much, thinking she needs to be sharp tomorrow, and nurses her beer. The firepit's going, the smokers gathered round on picnic benches and lawn chairs and stumps, watching sparks float up into the night sky. It takes her a second to recognize Ryan, dressed like a pirate, a stuffed parrot drooping on his shoulder. Hector says they should say hi to him, pay their respects. She knows he's just being polite, but sometimes he's like an old lady.

"Fuck," Ryan says, "you guys missed it. Fucking Benny and Doug-o threw down. It was fucking brutal, yo. They were standing there chilling and they just started going at it."

"There was blood everywhere," his girlfriend Lindsay says. She's also dressed as a pirate, but a sexy one, and seems too excited about the blood.

"What happened?" Hector asks.

"Benny kicked his ass."

"Why were they fighting?" Birdy asks, because that's what Hector meant.

"Who fucking knows. We thought they were just playing but they were fucking serious."

It's the big news, what the party will be remembered for, a highlight of their senior year. Later a rumor spreads that Doug-o had to go to the hospital and have his jaw wired. Another, which they hear repeated in the too-bright glare of the kitchen and then upstairs as they wait in line for the bathroom, is that the fight was over Casey Daigle, who broke up with Benny at the end of the summer, though no one thinks Doug-o ever got with her.

"Yeah," Birdy says, "I don't think so." Because Doug-o's nowhere near Casey's level—exactly what people would say about her and Myles.

"Maybe he said something," Hector says.

Birdy doesn't ask what that would be.

"Guys are idiots," Lisa Sansom says behind them.

"There you go," Birdy says, just as the door opens.

Hector wants to come in with her, but she pushes him back with one hand, earning a laugh, and locks the door. In the mirror she's guilty, bitter. Guys aren't the only idiots.

She checks her phone but there's only a text from Elena she's too tired to answer.

Gregory and Sonya are out. It's past midnight, but Hector wants another beer. He's fine to drive, he just doesn't want the party to end.

"One last one," she concedes, as if it's a negotiation.

On the stairs, as they're heading down into the writhing mass of the dance floor, a strobe catches the frozen profile of the girlfriend and goes black again.

It happens so fast that Birdy thinks she's imagined it, and slows, Hector bumping into her, almost bowling her over. She keeps going, holding on to the banister, watching the darkness, waiting for the next flash. When it blooms, making the walls of the room jump, she can see her clearly, her long hair swinging as she flings her head back and tips up her chin, giving Myles her throat, the two of them locked on each other in the middle of the crowd, then gone.

Birdy's first instinct is to run to him, her second to bolt for the front door and out into the night, but with Hector at her shoulder, all she can do is keep going, losing sight of them as she descends.

They retreat to the back porch. She doesn't want a beer. She wants to go home. She wasn't supposed to be here, and now she's angry with Hector and with herself, and, unfairly, with Myles. She doesn't want to see them together. He has to know that, after today. In an instant it's all ruined—the room, the view, the rain. Everything she thought they had is an illusion. He's popular and gorgeous and rich. She's a fool to think they could ever be together.

She fills her cup anyway, and they head across the yard to the firepit, which is packed, no seats anywhere. Lindsay is picking out the *Munsters* theme on a guitar. It's a game, people calling out songs, trying to stump her. "*Halloween*!" "*Scooby-Doo*!"

"Too easy," Lindsay says, and dashes them off.

Birdy can't stop seeing him dancing and gulps her beer, keeping one eye on the back door. The longer they stand there, the more certain she is that he'll come out and take the guitar from Lindsay, and then Birdy will have to listen to him sing for everyone and pretend she doesn't care. She sang for him today under the covers, her secret song. Now she thinks it was a mistake. She needs to protect that little girl.

She's almost finished with her beer, and knocks her cup against Hector's. "Drink up."

She's known him long enough to know he won't let her beat him. He tips his head back and chugs his down, foam dripping from his wispy excuse of a mustache, just as Lindsay calls out, "Are you ready, kids?"

"Aye aye, Cap'n!" the circle answers.

"I think we're leaving at the right time," Birdy says.

"I think so," Hector says.

The driveway goes around the house, so there's no need to go back inside. It's dark, only the glow from the kitchen window showing them the way, the music pounding through the walls. Someone's lost part of their costume, a wet lump of fabric balled on the ground, till they reach it and the shape resolves into a pair of panties.

"Someone had a party," Hector says.

"Someone's nasty."

Fog curls off the edge of the front porch. Beyond it, backlit by the coach light, is a huddle of people sharing a joint—Ryan with the parrot on his shoulder, a couple in full Mario and

Luigi costumes, and behind them, cups in hand, Myles and the girlfriend.

"You gone?" Ryan asks.

"We gone, bruh," Hector says, giving him a soul shake.

"A'ight. Drive safe."

Myles is busy hitting the joint, the ember flaring, coloring his face. As Birdy passes, she tries to catch his eye, but he turns from her, handing it to Luigi, who has to take off a glove and bow his head to see through his mask. Instead it's the girlfriend who's watching her, measuring her with a smirk, and Birdy looks away as if slapped, facing straight forward as they walk down the drive, hiding behind Hector, afraid to look back.

She understands that he was ignoring her on purpose. Still, it hurts. All she wanted was a sign—a nod, a wave, anything. He wouldn't even look at her. And the bitch, the fuck was she looking at? Birdy doesn't care if she's twice her size, the dumb heifer, she'll fuck her up.

Hector takes her hand, and it's all Birdy can do not to pull away.

The air's colder now. The road's moonlit and quiet, the music thumping faintly behind them. A lot of the other cars are gone, making the walk seem longer. She'll see him tomorrow—today, she thinks. Why isn't it enough? She thinks of him constantly and he won't even look at her. As they approach Hector's car, she's resigned to the idea that she loves Myles more than he loves her, and that it's probably always been that way for him. Lost in her thoughts, she's surprised to see the Charger's not out here by itself, and has to disguise a smile of triumph.

Across the driveway, parked so the two are facing each other like rivals, is his Eclipse.

The TV's on when he drops Angel off, a frame of light stuttering at the edges of the drapes. She's late and hasn't texted, and expects her mother will be drunk. During their worst fights, her mother calls her selfish and lazy—"a lazy, stupid girl who doesn't care about anyone but herself"—and the next day says she doesn't remember anything. Her mother cries and tries to apologize, explaining that she doesn't want her to end up like her, an argument Angel doesn't buy. She should be used to it, but each time she's stung by how little her mother thinks of her. No matter what she does, she's the pretty one, everything handed to her.

"You working tomorrow?" Myles asks.

"After church. Did you want to come?"

"I'm good."

Normally he's all over her, making her feel bad for having to say goodnight, but it's late and he lets her go with just a kiss.

"I'll call you tomorrow," he says, and backs out, then sits in the road, waiting while she finds her keys and opens the door. She waves to release him, and he rockets off, his muffler purring.

Stepping inside, she's prepared to defend herself, but no one's there to scold her, only macho voices from the TV. Maybe she's lucky and her mother's passed out. She creeps into the living room and finds Jean-Luc Picard fighting the Borg Queen, and Marie asleep on the couch in her pj's.

"Seriously," Angel says.

It's past one. She checks her phone but there are no messages. Her mother's always telling her to let her know if she's going to be late, but it doesn't work the other way around. She goes home with guys she's just met and doesn't show up until the next day, and it's okay because she's an adult. The one time Angel called her a slut, her mother slapped her hard and didn't apologize, and Angel understood why her father left her.

She doesn't have a number for Russ and has no clue where he lives. All she can do is text her mother to say she made it home and hope she gets it.

She finds the clicker and turns off the TV, rousting Marie, leading her up the stairs. By the time Angel gets her into bed, she's awake.

"How was the movie?"

"Stupid."

"You smell like smoke."

"There was a bonfire at the party."

"Was it fun?"

"Meh."

"Did you and Myles do anything else?"

"Like what?"

"I don't know."

"We danced."

"That's fun."

"It was," Angel says. "Now go to sleep."

"Where's Mom?"

"Don't worry about her, she's fine."

When they were little, she used to pretend Marie was her baby. Now, tucking her in, bending to kiss her forehead, she thinks that in some ways she still is. Who else will look out for her?

Downstairs she checks her phone, goes to the front door and peers out at the puddles on the driveway and the windowless hulk of the mill, as if any second Russ and her mother might pull up. She stands there with the cold air seeping through the glass as a lone car approaches, the glare of its headlights racing along the telephone wires in parallel, throwing the shadow of the guardrail into the weeds, and swishes past without slowing, leaving the road empty again. The wind rises, whistling around the house, rattling branches, stirring leaves. She could be the one in a Stephen King movie now, the good-hearted babysitter who fights off the unstoppable killer. She thinks of waiting up for her like Marie, but knows better. Her mother can take care of herself. She's probably having more fun than she is—either that or passed out. One last, pointless check of her phone and she turns off the porch light and slides the deadbolt home, locking the two of them in for the night.

Good Luch

I don't know if my mother was in love with Russ or just wanted to be with someone. It was always hard to tell. She was practical in everything but love. After Wes, she hadn't had anything steady and had gained weight, all mirrors her enemy. Angel said she was desperate. Having had nothing but hopeless crushes on TV stars, I couldn't argue with her. Wasn't all love desperate?

Neither of us liked Russ. He was old and fat and dressed like a teacher, with his class ring and gold watch. He drove too fast when he took us to the Wilcox Tavern in his Escalade, showing off, and made a point of pulling out a chair for our mother. He drank Manhattans instead of beer, and didn't eat his French fries, then paid like he was our father, waving the folder with the check at the waitress instead of waiting for her to take it.

"Well," our mother said, back at the house, "what do you think?"

She'd had a lot of wine, and neither of us wanted to answer.

"He doesn't seem like your type," Angel said.

"I know!" she said, as if she was surprised too. "It's really nice to be with someone who knows who they are. What do *you* think?"

I thought that I didn't want to share a bathroom with him.

"He's got a nice car," I said.

"It's huge, isn't it? I think he's doing okay for himself."

"What does he need a car that big for?" Angel asked, like he might have a secret family.

"He's a big guy."

"Have you tried stalking him on Facebook?"

"No."

"That's the first thing you've got to do."

"I doubt he's on it," our mother said, trying to discourage us, and she was right, he was too old for Facebook. All we found online were some local addresses and a LinkedIn page we couldn't open. His middle name was Pugh, which became a joke we used to annoy her—P.U., Poo, Winnie the Pugh.

Our grandmother had her doubts as well, but she didn't like any of our mother's boyfriends. As much as she disliked our father, she saw their divorce as a moral failing. She'd married our grandfather when she was eighteen and still laid a wreath at his grave every Christmas and Easter. He had brown lung from working for the Line & Twine his whole life, his bronchial tubes clogged with cotton dust, and in his final years rarely left his recliner, summoning her by slapping his cane against the side like a bass drum. He wasn't an easy person, she said, as if giving herself credit for staying with him. In her eyes, our mother had taken the easy way out, and every man she'd been with since had taken advantage of her.

Our father didn't have an opinion, or not one he shared with us. He'd first met our mother when he was doing landscaping at the Elms, and still did some work for them. During the week, while I was in school, it was possible that my mother or Aunt Mil might look out a window and see him trimming the hedges or clearing the lawn with a leaf blower, his earphones insulating him from the rest of the world. His appearances there were so common that my mother no longer mentioned them, and though I imagined her waving to him, or the two meeting cute along a newly edged walkway and exchanging pleasantries, I expect that more often than not my parents passed without speaking, like strangers.

For Angel and me, as daughters it was not our place to let our father know our mother was getting serious about someone else, and he didn't ask after her beyond a token, easily deflected "How's she doing?" at the beginning of our visits. His feelings were his, and if he shared any with us, they belonged to the past, memories of holidays and vacations, like snapshots in a family album. He was happy to see us, everything was going great, but his inner life was as mysterious to us as that of an extraterrestrial or creature of the deep. The walls of his apartment were bare, a masculine lack of effort we took as evidence of his sadness, like his mismatched silverware and empty refrigerator. We snooped through the place, poring over his blank calendar and short grocery lists, going through his wastebaskets, finding nothing but bottle caps and toenail clippings and expired coupons. We had so little of him, we always wanted more.

The Friday before Columbus Day, while we were eating scallion pancakes and General Tso's chicken at the Chinese place downstairs, our mother was out gallivanting with Russ, as our grandmother would say. It was impossible not to imagine them coming back to our house and Russ spending the night, the naked weight of him pinning our mother to her bed, yet the three of us sat talking about the Red Sox and the Patriots and Angel studying for her SATs like everything was fine. I was trying to be careful about what I ate but kept taking another gooey nugget of chicken, another greasy spoonful of fried rice, until the waitress came and asked if we wanted boxes for everything.

As the youngest, I had first pick of the fortune cookies. "You will overcome many obstacles."

"I'm sure you will," our father said.

Angel laughed at hers.

"What's it say?"

"You will be showered with good luch."

"Luch."

She showed us the typo. "I'm keeping this one. What does yours say?"

"Learn Chinese: Mustache. *Hu zi.*"

"No, the other side."

"All things come to him who waits."

"He," I said.

"It's better than luch," he said.

"Showered," Angel said. "That's how much luch I'm going to have."

"You sure it wasn't lunch? You're going to be showered with lunch."

We had so little to talk about that it became a catchphrase, an easy laugh, and Sunday, when he dropped us off, he wished us good luch at school that week, confusing our mother, who didn't think it was funny.

Inside, the house smelled, a briny, chemical mingling of Febreze and seafood. We'd grown so alert to the smallest clues that even before we set our bags down, Angel gave me a sideways look. Our mother asked how our weekend had been, and we turned the question back on her. She and Russ had gone to the casino Friday night, to the restaurant they liked. It was very nice. She didn't say she'd brought him home, as if all three of us didn't know. We waited to see if she'd explain the reek. When she didn't, we didn't press her, just took our bags upstairs and started our reconnaissance.

Though garbage night wasn't till Tuesday, our mother had emptied the bathroom wastebasket, leaving only a single string of floss. While Angel checked our mother's bedroom, I went downstairs to occupy her and make a swing through the kitchen. She'd taken out the trash, but by the basement door, in the recycling bin, stood a big bottle of her chardonnay. We'd routinely seen her kill one in the course of an evening, so it didn't mean anything. In the fridge was a box of leftovers from the restaurant, just the one—steak and mashed potatoes and creamed spinach.

That was Friday night, so Saturday she'd cooked for him, or maybe he'd cooked for her, since he was supposed to be this big foodie. I couldn't decide which was worse.

My mother was in the basement, flipping the laundry, when Angel came down and beckoned me with a finger to come upstairs.

She led me to our mother's bed, stripped of its sheets. By her nightstand, she leaned down close to the quilted mattress pad and naked pillows and sniffed, waving the fragrance under her nose like a chef, and motioned for me to do the same.

Woody and herbal with a bite of lime, the scent was familiar, a men's deodorant or body spray—not Axe, which the boys in my grade fogged on like bug repellent, but something cleaner.

"Old Spice Swagger," Angel said.

I turned to her as if I'd heard her wrong. "It's not Russ."

"It's . . ." She nodded slowly, coaxing the answer out of me like we were playing charades.

"Wes."

"It's Russ and *then* it's Wes."

"Ew."

I didn't want to picture it. I didn't know what our mother was doing. Russ we didn't like, but we were afraid of Wes. He owned guns and ninja throwing stars and did cocaine. In his truck, under the driver's seat, in case someone pissed him off, he kept a hammer. After our escape, I thought we'd never have to see him again.

Now the smell made sense. Later, when our mother went food shopping, we snuck out back where the garbage can stood against the falling-down garage. The can was in the sun, and as soon as Angel opened the lid, the deathly stink of day-old lobster hit us. The bag was right on top, lumpy with shells. She undid the twist tie and there were the red bodies with their antennas and legs, the cracked claws and mangled tails and fat rubber bands, along with a half dozen flattened Budweiser cans—his brand. For a moment we stood staring at the mess like detectives reading a crime scene, trying to scare up theories, then Angel twisted the bag closed again and shut the lid.

"Maybe it was someone else," I said.

"It was him," she said, as if I was being dumb. "Why does she do shit like this?"

If our mother suspected we knew, she didn't let on. When she came home, she put the groceries away and started dinner, humming to herself as she browned some onions, puzzling us further. As much as we dreaded her depressions, we distrusted her happiness more, as if she was deluded or overcompensating, bound to relapse.

"What else did you do without us?" Angel asked at the table. "Throw any wild parties?"

"It was actually pretty quiet around here."

"How many dates are you up to now, six?"

"Five."

"And?"

Our mother looked from Angel to me, to remind her I was listening. "A lady never tells. You should know that."

"I've got nothing to tell."

"That's good," our mother said. "Let's keep it that way."

It sounded like a challenge, a dig over some other, bigger secret I didn't know, possibly. I expected Angel to ask her straight out if she'd seen Wes, but she retreated—strategically, I thought. She'd given her every chance to confess, making her silence a lie. In our house, this counted as a victory.

If nothing else, it confirmed our suspicions. As always with our mother, we expected the worst. We waited for her to tell us she was breaking up with Russ and we were moving back to the duplex. Walking home from the bus stop, I knew that one day I'd find Wes's lifted pickup in the driveway and him sitting on our front steps, smoking and spitting on the ground between his feet. I'd even devised a plan to text Angel and hide from him inside the mill until she rescued me, but as the week went by, Wes never showed. I let myself in and made a plate of Ritz crackers and peanut butter and poured a tall glass of orange juice and did my algebra homework while watching *Maury*.

Friday, Myles came to pick up Angel, and Russ came to pick up my mother, leaving me alone, which I didn't mind. Sunday we went to church with our grandmother, then watched the Patriots win again. We weren't wrong about Wes, but with each passing day he seemed less of a threat, just another momentary lapse on our mother's part, a by-product of her drinking. Nothing had changed. At times I let myself think that maybe we were safe, yet even at my most wishful I didn't really believe it, while Angel, being older, and closer to her, never did. We feared drama but we were addicted to it too. Because we were young, we thought we were strong. We thought we were hardened. We wanted the bad thing to happen fast, for the painful moments to be over so we could go on with our normal, boring lives.

2

They can't be apart for long. Birdy meets him after school, after soccer practice, after work, wearing her uniform, her hair smelling like cheesesteaks, which he swears he loves. It still feels like a risk, getting in his car, but she doesn't care. They're beyond right and wrong, like criminals. They won't stop until they're caught.

The beach house is safe, but not the beach. There are too many people on the weekends, especially when it's sunny. They need to get out of town. They go north along the shore, up to Point Judith and Galilee, where the Block Island ferry docks. It's nice to sit in a restaurant and wander around the wharf together, part of the crowd. People treat them like any other couple basking on a Sunday afternoon. She's allowed to hang on his arm, to muss his hair and steal his sunglasses and pose by the railing with the fishing boats and seagulls behind her. Taking a selfie with him, cheek to cheek, she catches people watching them and imagines they're jealous. Deep down, she is too. This happiness is an act, the clock always ticking. Even here she daydreams of what life would be like if they were free. The ferry glides in and unloads, takes on a line of cars and departs again, blaring its horn, and she wishes they were on board, headed for open water. As the white dot grows smaller and smaller, she can't stop kissing him, marking her territory, and it's true. Now, if only for a few hours, he's hers.

The hardest part is when he drops her off. They always take his car, meaning she has to leave hers in a safe lot. The easiest is the Walmart in Dunn's Corners, so sprawling she sometimes forgets where she parked. They don't linger like they did at the beginning. He gives her a quick kiss, she closes her door, and once he's gone, she feels drained, the rest of the day meaningless. After Galilee, the regular world is ugly. Around her, shoppers bustle, pushing carts piled high with bags. The weekend's over, everyone's going home. The people look shabby to her—middle-aged, slump-shouldered, overweight. It seems impossible that any of them were ever beautiful or in love.

She ties her hair back like she's come from work, inspects her face and then shakes her head, frustrated by this other Birdy who has no clue what she's doing. He's sweet, but he doesn't belong to her. What does she think is going to happen?

They have their songs now—good or bad, anything they hear becomes their soundtrack—and she can't turn on the radio for fear of being ambushed. She drives in silence, chewing her lower lip, as if this is the only time she has to think, these in-between moments alone. She has no plan to win him beyond offering herself. She'll break up with Hector and let him know, and then whatever happens, happens. It isn't fair to Hector to go on like this, or to the girlfriend. By tomorrow these resolutions will have evaporated, given way to cowardice and common sense, to the ever-present temptation to text him, but for now, cruising past the stripped cornfields and farm stands hawking pumpkins and apple cider, trying to hold on to the fast-fading afternoon, she sees what she needs to do.

Home, her real world returns, with its inescapable obligations. Her mother is waiting for her, and Ofelia, leaping up on her, making her tell her to get down. Her mother just got off the phone with Josefina, and replays their conversation. Luz has gained two pounds this week, that jumper she made doesn't fit her anymore. On and on she goes, Ofelia sniffing Birdy's knees as if she knows where she's been. They love her, so why is she impatient with them? It's not quite dinnertime, and all she wants to do is close her door and go to sleep.

Upstairs, she opens the middle drawer of her desk and adds a packet of oyster crackers to the cigar box that belonged to her father. A guitar pick, an arcade token, a piece of sea glass, a champagne cork, an acorn, a tiny crab claw—each keepsake commemorates a date with Myles, as if she might forget them. The box is getting harder to close, and she gently shakes it to settle her treasure before slipping it back in the drawer. Later, dressed for bed, she'll take it out and paw through her talismans like a witch, as if she might enchant him with a spell. Sitting there with Ofelia, not knowing when she'll see him again, she wishes she believed in magic, and then her phone plinks, and it's Hector—*Sup*—though she just saw him last night, and she has to close the lid and set the box aside.

She needs to be careful with him. She doesn't think he suspects anything, but sometimes when they're together, she can't help it, she stops listening and drifts off. She knows she's being unfair. He's kind and reliable and honest, but all he talks about is baseball and cars and his dumb job. Maybe he feels the same way about her, complaining about Mr. Futterman and Sandra and her creepy customers. Maybe they've just been together too long.

They've had the same routine forever. Saturdays they go to the movies and then whatever party there is, get baked and end up parking in the woods by the golf course. It's always in the car, in the dark. There's no poetry, no champagne and candles. Lately she's made excuses, pushing his hands away, saying her stomach's upset, that she's had too much to drink, that it's too cold, but she can't always put him off, and rather than let him have her, she unzips him and bends to her work. She tries to get through it quickly, gripping him roughly, hurrying so it will be over. She closes her eyes and pictures Myles and afterwards feels sick. She is all the things her mother has taught her not to be.

"Thank you," Hector says, when she wishes he would just be quiet.

It's not his fault, yet instead of pity she feels disdain for him, a coldness that lasts well after he's dropped her off, as if he's wronged her. She brushes her teeth extra and cuddles Ofelia in bed, sniffling back tears. She's so fucked-up.

She tries to tell Elena some of what's going on, leaving out Myles.

"I just don't feel anything with him."

"Oh baby, I'm sorry," Elena says, and holds her.

"It makes me feel like I'm a bad person because I don't love him enough."

"It happens. People get tired of each other, even people who love each other. Maybe you need to take a break."

"Maybe we do," Birdy says, relieved to hear the solution spoken aloud.

"You think he knows?"

"I don't think so."

"You're probably right. He's not the sharpest."

"Don't make fun of him."

"You know what I mean."

"He's always been good to me."

"That makes it harder."

Birdy wants to ask how she should do it, though there's really no choice. Once they break up, they'll be the news around school, the target of rumors, who dumped who. That part seems easier than actually sitting down with him and telling him it's over. Can't she just change her relationship status?

She doesn't mention any of this to Myles Tuesday night when they talk on the phone. As always, they're their own favorite topic. The rest of the world doesn't exist. They're supposed to meet tomorrow after practice, both of them changing their schedules to steal a free hour in the middle of the week. He wants to take her out to dinner, but there's no place close where people won't see them.

"What about Golden Chopstix?" he asks, because it's tucked in back of a strip mall. "Nobody goes there."

"No one goes there because it's nasty."

"How about takeout? I could pick something up and meet you at the beach. It's supposed to rain."

She'll be late getting home, but she can picture the garage door rolling up and his car waiting in the other bay. "Sure."

"What do you want?"

"Not Golden Chopstix."

How easily he can make her happy. Just the anticipation of being with him is enough. The next morning it's pouring and gray out. In the shower she serenades Ofelia, belting out Rihanna. *Now that it's raining more than ever, know that we'll still have each other. You can stand with my Ofelia, felia, felia.*

"Someone's in a good mood for a change," her mother says, buttering a corn toaster cake, and Birdy squeezes her and kisses her cheek. "I'm guessing you and Hector made up."

Has she been that obvious? "No comment."

"I'm not saying anything. I just like hearing you sing."

Her mother likes Hector and will want to know why. How can Birdy explain when she doesn't understand it herself? These doubts don't help. Alone, in the right mood, she can believe everything will work out, then one wrong word and it all falls apart. Why does she have to defend her feelings as if they're not real?

At school she regroups, huddling in back by the smokestack with Hector and Elena and Roser and Gregory and Sonya, while

Myles hangs out front between the pillars with Ryan and his crew. Birdy knows his schedule by heart, smiles to herself each time she passes his locker. All morning, sitting in class, watching the rain fall on the tennis courts and the soccer field, she pictures their room at the beach, but then, after lunch, he texts to let her know he has to cancel. No explanation, just *sry.*

Her first instinct is to text him back and ask why—exactly what she shouldn't do. From the beginning she's expected they'll be found out, their fate decided by the tiniest slip. Now, if this is it, she thinks she's ready.

Every few minutes she checks her messages. If something happened, he'd tell her. She needs to trust him, and waits until the break before last period to text him back.

u ok, she asks.

He replies immediately: *work suuux*

In her disappointment, she thinks it's a lame excuse—doesn't he want to see her?—but writes *sry* and pockets her phone, vowing not to look at it till after practice. When she does, there's nothing, and she's too tired to be angry with him. She drives straight home and eats leftovers.

To punish him, she sets her phone on her desk to charge, turning off the sound so she won't hear it downstairs, where her mother's watching the playoffs. Like Hector, her mother loves the Yankees. "Catch it," she tells the players, as if they don't know what to do. They're winning, but Birdy's bored. When she tries to read a chapter of earth sciences, she can't concentrate and gives up.

When her father was alive, he used to take them to see the Norwich Navigators, a Yankees farm team a half hour away. While her mother and father watched the game, she and Josefina would play in the bouncy house down the left field line and eat ice cream and tag along after the mascot, Tater the Gator, who snuck up behind people on hot days and squirted them with a Super Soaker. Once, a bat flew out of a player's hands and was headed right for their section when her father stood up and caught it and everyone cheered. They let him keep it, and after the game he had some of the players sign it with a Sharpie. Now she wonders where it is. When her father died, her mother got rid of all his clothes except his Yankees gear and a pair of old slippers. Josefina thought it was random, but Birdy, with her cigar box, understood. If it had been up to her, she would have kept everything.

She gives her mother a kiss and heads up to brush her teeth.

Her phone says she has one new message.

raincheck? he asks.

The timestamp was two hours ago, so she's already made him wait.

when

fri, he fires back.

She almost wants to say no to teach him a lesson, except Saturday she's working and Sunday they have dinner at Josefina's, so it's her only chance to see him this weekend. She has to see Hector no matter what, and is dreading it. She's already sorry she told Elena about them.

k, she replies, and thinks she should be happy, but she's tired and cross with herself and then can't sleep.

The next morning, as she and Elena are changing classes, she passes him in the hallway with the girlfriend, who seems taller somehow, more powerful. She's pale, with dark lipstick, almost goth, her hair perfectly straight, as if she's ironed it. She's long-limbed, like a model, where Birdy's petite. Beside her, Birdy feels like a child. He sees Birdy, and before he can stop himself, starts to smile, and she has to force herself to ignore him and keep walking and not say anything to Elena.

The temptation is to text him or slip a note in his locker. If she wanted to blow things up, that would be the fastest way. Sometimes she thinks it would be easier, but she's afraid he might get mad at her. She won't risk losing him by doing something stupid. She needs to take care of her own shit first, and she can't even tell Hector.

Friday after practice she's supposed to meet Myles at the beach. She's told her mother that she's going out for pizza with her teammates and might be late. She's lied to her dozens of times now, she's never around, so why does the thought of her mother eating alone bother her? Josefina was the wild teenager, totaling her car, getting pregnant. Birdy's always been the good girl, and feels split in two. While she's honestly shocked at her own heartlessness, she has no plans to stop.

All day she waits for him to text her and say he can't make it. Even after practice, turning her phone on again, she expects a message, but there's nothing. The days are growing shorter. It's fully night by the time she reaches the beach, the stars sharp, the lot empty except the two RVs, their windows yellow against the dunes. When she pulls in, the house is dark. Sitting in the drive, she thinks she's made a mistake, that something's wrong. She reaches for her phone, and the door rises like a curtain, shedding light, and there he is, barefoot, with a glass for her. Everything's fine.

"Oh my God," she says, clinging to him. "This has been the longest week."

Friday it's date night, finally. She and Russ have the whole evening. He likes the casinos with their trendy restaurants and bumping dance clubs, a miniature Vegas hidden in the woods of Connecticut. If they drink too much they can always get a hotel room, an extravagance that never fails to impress Carol. Checking into a suite feels like a vacation, like they could be anywhere. After being on her feet all day, she loves sitting in a jacuzzi with a chilled glass of wine, letting the heat melt away her aches, the clean sheets like velvet against her skin. If Russ isn't Wes in bed, Wes never treated her like this either.

"It's cheap," Russ says. "Plus I get points on my Wampum card."

Tonight he has tickets to Cirque du Soleil, which she's told him she's wanted to see. They order cocktails, but the service is slow, the show is strange and endless, and when the lights come back up they're both headachy. She still hasn't seen his place, so when he suggests they go there, she agrees, trying not to seem too eager.

They drive south down 78 toward the shore, crossing the Post Road, going straight past Angel's CVS. He's said it's a condo, which could mean anything—a new townhouse in Watch Hill with a deck overlooking the harbor, or the ones right on the golf course in Weekapaug, popular with snowbirds. The closer to the ocean, the more expensive things are. Something on an inlet would be nice, a dock at the bottom of the yard. She knows she's being shallow, and tries not to get her hopes up, but there's so much waterfront down here. Is it wrong to want something better than where they are? It's not like she could ever afford it herself. How many chances like this will she get?

At Shore Road he turns left, so they're not going all the way, but close. There are farms and golf courses along here, a few old motels and B&Bs with views across the salt ponds. The Escalade takes the curves and dips like a roller coaster, its headlights flitting over stone walls and stands of beach roses. Just before the racquet club, Russ slows, signals. She's convinced he's going to turn in, but he overshoots the entrance and takes the next one, marked with a simple knee-high sign: *Private*. It's only as they wind uphill through an apple orchard that they pass a carved green-and-gold oval framed by brick pillars and spotlit, announcing *The Mews at Champlin Woods, An Active Adult Community*.

"It's true," he says. "I live at the Home."

Her first thought isn't how old he must be, but how new the place is, how pricey. She knows people who work there, lured away from the Elms by higher pay and better benefits. Like a lot of senior centers, it offers everything from independent living to memory care. The idea is that once you go in, you don't come out.

"How is it?"

"It's nice. The food could be better, but I do most of my own cooking."

She can think of a few reasons he didn't tell her. Having had him to her house, she feels duped, but she can't completely blame him. People are weird about money.

They have to stop at a gatehouse. The guard who comes out with a clipboard looks old enough to be a resident and calls Russ by his first name.

"So, you going to introduce me?" the guard asks.

"Carol, Kenny. Kenny, Carol."

"Nice to meet you," she says.

"Heard a lot about you—all good."

"That's good."

"Well, I'll be seeing you."

After he's raised the bar for them to go through, she asks Russ, "What was that all about?"

"He's just a chatterbox. He chats everyone up."

"He's heard a lot about me, apparently."

"Not from me he hasn't. He'll remember your name though. He writes them down so we'll tip him at Christmas."

On their dates she's so used to having him to herself that it's strange to meet someone who knows him, even casually. She wants to go back and ask Kenny questions, take notes. This is Russ's world. She feels like she needs to memorize it, as if she might see it only this once.

Evenly spaced along the ridgeline, the three main buildings look like beach hotels, four stories each with balconies that face the sea. His is the middle one. In the foyer, he has to punch in a code to enter, and there, across from the elevators, is the same bank of mailboxes they have at the Elms, a recycling can beside it for the residents to ditch their junk mail. By the elevator, taped to the wall, a flyer advertises a Halloween party in the Commons. He has to slide a card into a slot before hitting the button for his floor—four.

"The penthouse," she says.

"It was all they had when I applied—at least that's what they said. I don't know if I believe that."

The hall on his floor is empty and quiet and the same slightly raised temperature as at her work. The walls are a neutral beige, but the residents have personalized their doorways with meaningful objects—a golf-themed welcome mat, a brass umbrella stand, a ceramic cat planter with flowing ivy growing out of its back. Again, they could be at the Elms, and she feels awkward in her cocktail dress, as if any second Mrs. Landrum or Aunt Mil might round the corner.

Beside his door hangs an old-fashioned Japanese scroll, people with umbrellas crossing a bridge in the rain, nothing she'd associate with him—or anyone, really—and she's discouraged by how little she knows him, like she hasn't been paying attention.

Entering his apartment feels more intimate than checking into a hotel room, more serious, as if she's trespassing. On the walls, on the mantel, everywhere are pictures of his children and grandchildren—with or without him, at the beach or skiing, playing tennis, riding horses, dressed for a wedding, posing on the steps of some tropical resort. It shouldn't be a surprise. He's told her about his family all along, yet she still sees him as a single guy like her other boyfriends, unreliable, terrified of responsibility. She's not sure if she wants to believe he's different, even if he is.

This must be the ex-wife with their daughter's wedding party, a curvy brunette with big teeth and an '80s poodle perm. Carol thinks she's probably closer in age to the daughter. How long have they been divorced? Do they talk like her and Frank, or do they hate each other?

"What would you like?" he asks from the kitchen. "I make a mean Manhattan."

"That sounds good," she says, trying to figure out whether the leather couch and matching chair came from a house or he bought them special for this room. She wonders how long he's been here. To apply you have to be fifty-five. She's forty-two, middle age a good decade away. She still thinks of herself as young, even if that's not true anymore.

It's only a one-bedroom, and the kitchen's tiny. The balcony's nice, and the gas fireplace. Though she knows it costs a fortune, compared to their house it seems small and sterile, a downsized life. Was she really hoping he'd have room for her and the girls?

"I like it," she says. "It's cozy."

"Thank you. It's cookie-cutter, but it serves its purpose."

The drink revives her, boozy and bittersweet, reminding her that it's just a date. He puts on some jazz and cuts the lights so they can take in the view. It's cold out on the balcony. He uses it as an excuse to hold her from behind, pointing out the dark blots of Fishers Island and the North Fork, and to the south, tiny, all by itself on the horizon, winking every few seconds, the light at Montauk. She's more impressed with the sweep of the night sky, salted with constellations, how the half moon and brighter stars draw her eye. The more she looks, the more stars there are, galaxy after galaxy, infinite, she imagines, a kind of promise. She's been gazing at them her whole life and doesn't know their names. In the presence of so many, she feels very small and alone in the universe, despite his arms around her.

"Listen," he whispers, and after a time she can make out the waves, a mile away, falling on the shore as regular as breath.

"I hear it."

He kisses her neck and she lifts her chin and grips the railing, still watching the stars, unsure what to wish for.

Birdy's in bed, texting late with Elena, venting, when she receives an auto message that the Runaway Bunny has tagged her in a photo. It's a joke page for the whole school, named after the statue in Wilcox Park where people cut class. Everyone's friends with it. She figures the post is from Gabriela's party earlier that night, a group shot of their crew in costume, Hector and her dressed as Batman and Catwoman, but when she goes to the page, the picture is from last weekend, from Galilee. The ferry is a white blob in the background as she and Myles—facing away from the camera—stand at the railing, holding hands.

"No," she says, sitting up, waking Ofelia. "No, no, no."

She's tagged. He isn't.

The post just popped, but there are already comments.

Dat lil ho!

Bitch b funsize

MP da Mack

"Fuck."

srsly, Elena texts, the balloon cutting off their heads, *nobody likes her*

Birdy swipes her away and untags herself, knowing it's too late, pissed at whoever did this. Though she's not entirely surprised, she's hurt to discover she has enemies. Even if her friends won't see the post immediately, eventually the whole school will. This isn't how she wants Hector to find out.

First she needs to tell Myles. As she's deciding whether to call or to text him, another auto message pops: *Jordan Washburn has tagged a photo of you.*

"Stop," she says, untagging it.

Allie Marrone has tagged a photo of you.

She changes her settings so no one else can do it, though the requests keep rolling in.

Sam Larkin has tagged a photo of you.

Nicole Perry has tagged a photo of you.

The frenzy's on. They must be underclassmen, because she doesn't recognize their names. She's been expecting something like this for weeks, but it's still a shock. With no one to blame, it feels almost impersonal, the work of trolls.

WTF, Elena asks, with the photo attached, and any hope Birdy might have had vanishes. Their Sunday road trips and meetings at the beach—that sweet, secret time is over.

sry, she says. *mnt to tell u gtg ttyl*

She calls Myles but gets a busy signal and the prompt for his voicemail.

Her phone vibrates and it's Elena. She has to accept.

"Why didn't you tell me? I mean, I get it now, I should have figured it out, but you could have fucking told me."

"I'm sorry," Birdy says. "I couldn't. Look, I can't talk right now. I need to call Myles."

"You haven't talked to him yet?"

"I'm pretty sure he's talking with her."

"Yeah. Jesus. What about Hector?"

"I've gotta go. I'm sorry."

"Okay. Love you, chica."

"Love you too."

Myles is still busy, so she texts him: *need to talk*

The answer takes a while, and then it's just: *tomorrow*

She doesn't understand. She should be the one he's talking to, not her.

ily, she tries because she needs a sign from him. She wonders if he called the girlfriend or she called him, and what each of those would mean. She doesn't really want to talk to Hector. The last time she broke up with someone was with Matt Yu in ninth grade, and they're still friends.

Myles is typing, typing, and then for a while the icon disappears. The notifications keep pouring in, everyone commenting, piling on, calling her a slut, a spic, a midget.

Ily to, he says, and with both hands she clutches the phone to her chest and falls back into her pillows, scaring Ofelia.

It's all Birdy needs. It gives her the courage to call Hector. Just a few hours ago they were in his car at the golf course, making out with the seats down. Now she feels like she's escaped. So why does she feel sorry for him?

His phone rings once, twice, three times. She imagines him declining the call—it's what she'd do—but then he picks up and doesn't say anything.

In the past, when they'd argue, he'd go silent on her, as if fighting was beneath him. He always thought he was right and never apologized. She can hear the clatter of a train in the background that makes her think he's outside, and for a moment she's afraid his car's parked right across the street. She's tempted to go to her window and see.

"Hey," she says.

Nothing.

"I'm sorry," she says. "I don't blame you for not wanting to talk to me. I wouldn't."

What does she need to say to him? What stops her from hanging up?

"I just want to say I'm sorry, that's all. This isn't how I wanted things to be."

The train barrels louder. Maybe he's stepped out on his back porch to smoke. His parents are sleeping, his brother and sister, the whole house except him, standing in the cold, looking at the woods.

"Okay," she says, to let him know she's going.

"Why?" he asks, surprising her.

It's too big of a question. "I don't know."

"You have to have some idea."

She could say it's because he's boring and Myles isn't. When she's with Myles, just doing nothing, she's happier than she ever was with him, every particle of her charged, the two of them fully connected, but even that's not it. How can she explain what she doesn't understand herself?

Now it's her turn to be quiet.

"I thought you were better than this," Hector says.

"I'm not."

He lets her answer linger, as if that's all he wanted from her—as if this admission is new. She doesn't need him to tell her she's a horrible person. She could have told him that months ago. Maybe she should have. Would it have made any difference?

"Okay," she says, and this time he doesn't stop her. She hesitates as if there's more to say, but there's just the train clacking, and that's it, she hits end and they're done forever.

It's only then, when no one but Ofelia can hear her, that she cries, wiping away the tears with both hands. She should be relieved—this is what she's wanted—but it's too much. Her phone is still blowing up and she turns it off, shutting out the noise of the world. She should probably take her page down.

What will she tell her mother and Josefina? She knew it would end like this, she just thought they had longer. The funny thing is that it's actually a sweet picture of them. She wouldn't mind a screenshot. It's past two and she's exhausted, but sleep is impossible. She lies in bed in the dark, counting the hours, waiting for her life to change.

In church Angel doesn't feel like confessing. She needs to hold on to her anger, not offer it up to God. She kneels between her grandmother and Marie, head bowed, mouthing the words, their meaning too pointed to ignore. *We have sinned against you in thought, word, and deed.* She's guilty of all three, but what he's done is much worse, a betrayal she fears she will never forgive, despite what she told him last night.

The person she's angriest with is herself, for being so blind. She had no idea he could lie to her like that. She didn't think she missed any obvious signs, but she doubts herself now, second-guesses her happy memories. She thought everything was fine, because she trusted him. It's not a mistake she'll make again. He promised he wouldn't talk to the little bitch anymore, but from now on he better know she'll be checking his phone.

They rise, cleansed, and Reverend Ochs bestows the Peace. They greet one another in their new, immaculate state, then sit through the announcements. Are there any newcomers with us this morning?

This isn't the first time he's cheated, she guesses, though she has no evidence to prove it. He swears it was just a hookup, nothing real. She doesn't care—he shouldn't even be looking at other girls. She may be wrong, but she blames the bitch more. Guys are stupid. They can't resist it when you shove it in their face. The bitch knew he was taken and she pursued him anyway, breaking the first rule. For that trespass, she needs to pay.

Three years they've been together. Did he really believe she'd just let him go after so long? Did he honestly think she wouldn't fight for him? Since their talk, the same thoughts keep revolving in her mind. Does he not know her at all?

She processes to the front with the rest of the congregation for Communion, helping her grandmother kneel and get to her feet again, and then with a final blessing the reverend releases them.

"Thanks be to God," they respond, and stand in line to shake his hand before returning to the world. One of the Proctor boys yanks off his tie and races across the parking lot, shirttails flying. She hadn't wanted to go. Now she's glad she did. Just by sitting through it she feels like she's accomplished something.

She has less than half an hour to get ready, once they get home, and feels rushed. She needs to be irresistible without being obvious. It's not that difficult—she knows what he likes—but after last night she's uncertain of her powers, and spends too much time deciding on the exact right top, her bed strewn with rejects. They're going to be outside, so she pulls her hair back into a ponytail and dabs on some lip gloss, Marie watching her from the doorway.

"Where are you guys going?"

"The beach."

"When will you be back?"

"I don't know. Why? What's happening later?"

"Nothing," Marie says, glum. "I just wondered."

"Go do something with Brookie. I'm sure she's not doing anything."

"Brookie's not allowed in the mill."

"Go down to the river then, or the cemetery."

"She can't go there either."

"Where *can* she go?"

"She can go in the backyard."

"Then do something in the backyard with her. You know she'll be happy to see you."

"She smells," Marie says, which is true. Besides having severe Down syndrome, Brookie exudes an eye-watering B.O. that makes people change seats on the bus.

"That's nice. You know what, do what you want, I don't care." She's done, and stows her makeup bag under the sink and pushes past her.

Marie trails her like a dog. "I don't want to watch stupid football."

"Then don't."

"That's all they do all day."

"Don't care don't care."

"You suck."

"You suck."

"Will you be back for *The Simpsons*?" Marie asks, so pathetic that Angel stops shoving things in her purse and holds up her right hand as if taking an oath.

"I will be back for *The Simpsons*. Happy now?"

"No."

"Okay." Before she forgets, she grabs two Sharpies from her desk, figuring at least one of them will work.

From out front comes a double honk. He's early, a good sign.

"Where are you two going?" her mother asks.

"Oh my God," Angel says. "We're going to the beach."

"I'm just asking. There's no need to bite my head off."

"We're going to the beach. The beach is where we're going. To the beach. Beach."

"Goodbye," her mother says.

Fuck you too.

"Hey," Myles says, tentative, not leaning in for a kiss, which she thinks is right. Let him wait.

It's not just him. The car is ruined, and his stupid fruity air freshener. How many times did the little bitch sit in the same seat she's sitting in? Without a word, she makes a fist and punches him as hard as she can in the bicep. He shies away and rubs it as if it hurts, signaling by his silence that he understands he deserves worse.

"Just drive," she says.

"Where?"

"Where do you think?"

She needs him to be honest now about everything and is relieved when he takes 78 for the beach. He knows where they have to go. As they ride along, she's turned almost sideways with her back against the door, as if holding a gun on him.

"Did you talk to her today?"

"No."

"Did you text her, did you e-mail her, did you contact her in any way?"

"You told me not to."

"That doesn't mean anything, obviously."

"I didn't."

"How do I know you're not lying to me?"

"Because I'm not."

"Where's your phone?"

"In my pocket."

She holds out her palm, and he arches his body off the seat to comply.

"Did you delete anything?"

Why is this a surprise to him? "I did."

"How much? A lot?"

"Yes." No hesitation, which she appreciates.

"Is her number still in here?"

"No."

"It better not be. Pictures?"

"No."

"What does that mean?"

"There aren't any pictures."

"*Were* there pictures?"

His face gives it away, and yet he seems to want some sort of credit for getting rid of them, as if, by this sacrifice, he's proven his loyalty. This is what he needs to learn. He was wrong. He will always be wrong. No matter what happens from now on, she will never feel sorry for him ever again.

"How many were there?"

"Not many."

"Did you take them yourself or did she send them to you?"

"She sent them to me."

"You didn't take any."

"I didn't."

She can't tell if he's lying, which means he probably is. He's taken pictures of her she wouldn't want anyone else to see, so why wouldn't he do it with someone else? She tries not to imagine the ones the bitch sent him.

She dumps the phone in the cupholder. "I don't want to hear her name. I don't want to see her face. I don't want you thinking about her. If you want to be with me, you need to be with me. It's that simple."

"I'm sorry."

"You can't just say sorry. That's not how it works. I don't think you're sorry at all."

"I am."

"Shut up. You're sorry you got caught. You weren't going to tell me. You were just going to let it go on until something happened, weren't you?"

He says nothing.

"Thanks," she says. "That really makes me feel great."

She can see he wants to say he's sorry again but fears he'll set her off. At least he doesn't try to defend himself. If he did, that would be it, she'd tell him to stop the car and let her out. Instead, they ride in silence past the CVS and the airport and down through the empty summer rentals, the approach and the first view of the sea no longer thrilling, and again she sees the two of them at the railing, holding hands. What haven't they taken from her?

It's an okay day, partly cloudy with a light wind, and the lot of the state beach has a scattering of cars, a cluster around the bathhouse. For a moment Angel wishes she were alone, that she didn't have to salvage this mess all by herself—and for what? Next year he'll be gone, off to URI, yet she can't let him go. She needs to make it clear. It's his weakness that's brought them here, not hers.

The first time he took her to the house, she'd been impressed, and not because of the location or the view. With its brand-new stainless-steel appliances and walk-in closets, it was nicer than any place they'd ever lived. She couldn't believe his family used it only in the summer. The few times she stayed with them, putting out the flags on the top deck in the morning or looking over their stretch of beach at sunset, she felt a pride of ownership she'd never known before, as if its glory somehow reflected on her. Now, climbing the stairs to his parents' room, she sees that it was never hers. Like the day-trippers at the state beach, she was always just a guest, easily replaced.

She sets her purse on his mother's night table, reclaiming the space.

"I bet you had the fire going, didn't you," she asks, opening the curtains so the light spills in. "Make one. I'll wait."

As they undress, separated by the bed, she's casually checking his body for bites and scratches, any mark she needs to erase. Too soon, he slips under the covers as if suddenly modest. She flings them off and grips him, throws a leg over and climbs on top, holding down his shoulders.

How he kisses her, what he says—everything is a test.

"Did you use protection?" she asks when it's time.

"Yes."

"At least you did something right."

When did they last make love during the day? She thinks it's telling that she can't remember. Her mistake was ever letting him out of her sight.

"Close your eyes," she says, and then gives his face the finger to make sure before wrapping both hands around his windpipe. She doesn't squeeze, just presses gently with her thumbs, in total control, wondering if she'd be strong enough. Probably, if he didn't resist.

He doesn't. While she rides him, he keeps his eyes closed without her having to tell him again, the two of them meeting faster and faster. She takes her hands from his throat to lean back and a coaster from the night table clatters to the floor. He reaches for her breasts—to her annoyance, his favorite part of her. As a reward, or reinforcement, she lets him. In the past, this is when she'd urge him on. Now she stays silent, listening to his breathing, keeping pace, driving down on him as he arches higher and higher and then seizes beneath her, his head tipped back. If there were a knife in her purse, she could draw it across his throat in one motion and they'd be done.

"Keep your eyes closed," she says, climbing off him.

"Okay." But hesitant—a question, almost a joke.

She fishes in her purse until she finds a Sharpie. She kneels over him—he's wilting, the condom only half on—and uncaps the marker. When the tip touches his skin, he flinches.

It works. The line's dark and thick, the smell intoxicating.

"What are you doing?"

"Shhh," she says. "Don't move or you'll ruin it."

Below his tan line, across his last ab, in giant black letters, she writes: **I ♥ AO**

"Almost done."

She plucks off the condom and holds him upright with a fist while she frames the shot with her phone—not perfect, but good enough.

"Okay, you can open them."

"Wow," he says in disbelief.

"You don't like it? I can do something else if you want."

"No, this is good."

"Now I'd like to go somewhere."

The helpless look he gives her is perfect. He thought he was done paying today. "Where?"

"Where do you think?"

On the way up she shoots a bunch of selfies of them in the car so whoever she asks to take their picture later won't have to see his dick.

"Smile," she says. "Pretend we're having fun."

Brookie doesn't understand Clue. There are too many characters and rooms and murder weapons to keep track of, but she loves playing anyway. She rolls and moves her purple token square by square through Tudor Mansion with no strategy beyond taking the secret passages, like it's Chutes and Ladders. "Secwet passage to study," she reads, beaming, and jumps her piece to the opposite corner with a flourish as if she's won. She's always amazed when Marie solves the case, though with only the two of them playing, the solution's obvious. Marie might as well be playing by herself, and is aware that without Brookie she would be.

Marie would rather be exploring the mill or following the river upstream to the oxbow below the cemetery with its silty beach where the older kids make fires at night, leaving behind their charred beer cans and empty cigarette packs like artifacts, but if something happened and they got caught, Mrs.

Tidwell would never let Brookie come over again. Marie's tired of being alone and likes being seen as trustworthy, she just wishes Brookie was less of an obligation and more of an actual friend. If she were babysitting, at least she'd get paid. Still, it's better than being at her grandmother's, listening to her and her mother argue over things that happened before she was born. Sunday is so boring.

"Mr. Gween," Brookie guesses. "In the study. With the wope."

Marie shows her the study card again and the rope. So it's Mr. Green in the conservatory with the lead pipe, Marie just needs to get there. Three turns later she does, and makes her accusation.

"Unh-uh," Brookie says, smiling and shaking her head, and turns over the lead pipe.

"I asked you that."

"Nuh-uh."

"I did." Marie shows her where it's checked off on her score pad. "So it has to be the candlestick. Let's see."

She opens the envelope and she's right again, mystifying Brookie.

Outside it's starting to get dark, and Marie has to walk her back down the road to her house, so she folds up the board and they put everything away. Scattered about the bottom of the box like receipts are old scoresheets of Angel's and their mother's, their handwriting recalling games played in other places, other times, the three of them always together. When she was little, she could never beat Angel, and thinks she knows how Brookie feels.

It's cold out, and Marie helps Brookie zip up her coat. The Tidwells live just five houses down, but, minding her mother's advice, Marie locks the front door behind them. There's no sidewalk, no curb, the grass matted and slippery with fallen leaves. As she does when they walk to the bus stop, Brookie takes her hand, and Marie hopes no one driving by will see them. They tromp along past the Line & Twine's company houses with their broken windows and ivy-swallowed garages, each a haunted version of their own. Across the road, the mill is one long wall bombed with half-assed graffiti. Despite the wind, Marie can hear the river flowing over the dam and wishes she didn't have to go to school tomorrow.

Mrs. Tidwell's beater is in their driveway, meaning she's back from food shopping. Even before she opens the door, Marie can smell cookies baking. It's one reason Brookie is so big. Mrs. Tidwell's even bigger, triple-chinned, rolls on rolls jiggling beneath her housedress. More than once, scolding Marie for overeating, her mother has warned her that she doesn't want to be like those two.

"Thank you, Marie," Mrs. Tidwell says, accepting Brookie from her. "Come get a cookie while they're hot."

Marie just wants to leave, to be done, but the warm smell of vanilla is too much, she can't think of a polite excuse, and ends up in their kitchen, ruining her dinner with cookies and milk. By the time she leaves, the streetlights are on.

"Thank you so much, Marie," Mrs. Tidwell says, overly grateful, because she can't afford to pay her.

"See you tomorrow, Brookie."

"See you tomowow." Brookie waves from the doorway.

Alone, trudging along in the dark, Marie shakes her head. Once Angel leaves, how different from the Tidwells will she and her mother be? Because, while she'd never say it to her mother's face, she doesn't believe in Russ. Nearby, a pickup truck thunders, ripping down the straightaway of Potter Hill Road. The wind rises and the shadows hurry her home.

Birdy can't believe he'd ghost her like this, total radio silence. All day she's been waiting to hear from him—a call, a text, anything to let her know what's going on. With the flood of comments pouring in, she's taken down her page. It's Elena who has to tell her about the shot of him and the girlfriend in the exact same pose—a surprise attack that wounds and confuses Birdy.

So that's why he couldn't answer her.

She doesn't know what to believe. She thought today would be a celebration. She did what she was supposed to. For whatever reason, he didn't. Now she wants to get on and see the picture herself, as if with further inspection she might be able to make sense of it.

"What are people saying?"

"People are assholes," Elena says, evading the question. Birdy waits her out. "They think it's funny, like she's dunking on you or something. I think she's crazy bananas, doing something like that. That takes some planning."

"It's a message."

"It's a message that says I'm crazy as fuck. You need to be careful with her."

"I don't care about her."

"What is he telling you?" Elena asks, fishing, and Birdy doesn't have an answer.

"It's not going to be easy," Birdy says. "We knew that."

"Sonya's telling everyone you broke up with Hector."

Birdy hasn't even told her mother yet. Now she has to before the news reaches Josefina. "What does she care? She doesn't even like Hector."

"I'm just telling you."

She wants to say it's none of Sonya's business, but it doesn't matter. By tomorrow everyone's going to know anyway. Why did she think Sonya would be a better friend to her? Gregory and Hector are like brothers, and Hector's done nothing wrong, so Birdy kind of understands. She's not used to people talking shit about her, whether she deserves it or not. At least she still has Elena.

"And you," she tells Ofelia, scratching her behind the ears. "Even if you do have nasty fish breath."

Downstairs, her mother's watching the Yankees, drinking a can of beer and knitting something pink for Luz. They're winning again, and Birdy doesn't want to ruin the mood. She'll try again in the morning, when she can break the news and take off without having to discuss it too deeply. She puts Ofelia out one last time, kisses her mother goodnight and goes up.

She's still hoping he'll call—they've talked way later than this, turning over their situation—and keeps her phone on her nightstand, checking it each time the screen blooms with a notification, but it's just Elena, continuing their conversation by herself and then forwarding a screenshot of the picture.

There they are at the railing, holding hands, the ferry a white blot behind them. It's not photoshopped, as she'd first hoped. She knows his Bruins hoodie, remembers wrapping her arms around him from behind, slipping her hands into the fleecy front pouch and pressing her cheek against his back, smelling his clean smell. The girlfriend's almost as tall as he is. She's on the volleyball team, and in regular classes like him, not AP like Birdy. Birdy's curious but at the same time doesn't want to know her too well. She enlarges the shot with her thumb and forefinger, as if that might change the meaning, but it just blurs.

What is she supposed to do with this?

She ignores Elena and forwards it to him—*wtf*—and lies down again, wondering if that was a mistake.

Downstairs, her mother cheers, and Birdy rolls over, thinking she's lost everything. Despite being exhausted, she knows she won't sleep, and when she finally does, Ofelia wakes her, licking her paws in the dark, making Birdy scold her and then check her phone. It's only three-thirty, and for the rest of the night she's up and down, finally dropping into a complicated dream of her father and a rental car, the two of them getting lost on the way to a foreign airport just before her alarm goes off.

There's nothing from him, and she scrolls back to his last message, *ily to*, as if to verify it actually happened. Technically, that was yesterday. What's changed since then? Is it just the girlfriend not wanting to give him up? Birdy doesn't understand her.

It's why she needed to be honest with Hector. If someone doesn't want to be with you, why do you want to be with them? She's done what she had to do. The rest is up to Myles.

The Yankees won again, and over breakfast Birdy lets her mother recap the highlights before telling her about Hector. She doesn't admit it was part of a larger plan, just says they've broken up.

"Why?" her mother asks, taking her hand, concerned, as if they were perfect for each other.

"A lot of reasons. It was going to happen eventually. It's better this way."

"I'm sorry. I thought you were happy. The other day I heard you singing, and I thought, Oh good, she's happy again. Because for a while you were unhappy."

Birdy expects Josefina will tell her mother everything, but for now, knowing they've broken up is enough.

"I haven't been happy with Hector for a long time," she says, and as she says it, it feels true. It's probably why she fell for Myles.

"I worry about you."

"Don't. I'm okay."

"I can't help it," her mother says, "you're all I have left," and holds her a moment before letting her go.

"I know you liked him."

"It doesn't matter what I like. You're the one who has to be happy with him."

Why was she worried? Her mother will always try to understand her. It's Josefina who'll give her shit.

In her rush to escape, she's early, and has to kill fifteen minutes in the lot of the Bess Eaton on Granite Street so she won't have to see anyone at the smokestack. She's tempted to not go at all, to keep driving by the traffic cop in his optic-yellow vest waving cars into the entrance and swing down to the beach, but that might be worse.

Because she's made herself late, she has to park at the far end of the lot. Walking back toward the rear doors, she sees his Eclipse head-in against the fence of the soccer field. She could detour and leave a note under his wipers or jammed in the doorframe, but there's no point. Their secret's out, the people have already voiced their opinion. By showing up today, she's daring everyone to say it to her face. As she nears the building with its rows of windows, she imagines the whole school watching her. She resists waving, or giving them all the finger.

The halls are weirdly empty. She has to go to the office to get a slip. Monday's an A day, meaning she has Mr. Calderon's earth sciences first. When she opens the heavy door, every face turns to her, including Sonya's, annoyed, as if Birdy's done something to her personally. Some guy in back snickers at a crack, and Birdy tries to pretend she doesn't hear and takes her seat in the middle, aware that people are staring. She pulls out her notebook and sets her backpack on the floor. When she looks up, Lexi Parenti, two rows over, glances away as if caught.

She focuses on Mr. Calderon, listing types of ecosystems on the board, but can't concentrate on what he's saying. Beside her notes from Friday, she's doodled a rose she doesn't recall drawing. Friday seems so long ago. Nobody knew about them then, and for a moment she drifts into nostalgia for that lost time.

"Right here in Westerly we have deciduous forest, meadow, freshwater ponds, wetlands, estuary. What else?"

Ocean. It's obvious, but she can't say it, and waits till Dani Lefebvre answers.

"What's special about the ocean here in Westerly? What conditions does it have as an ecosystem that make it different from other parts of the North Atlantic?"

Again, Birdy knows, but her best defense is silence. If she can't blend in with them anymore, she can at least not actively attract attention. As a strategy it works, but it makes class take forever.

Watching the minutes tick off, she imagines what she could say to Sonya that would fix things. She can't say she's sorry, because she's not. And Sonya's the one going around telling people she broke up with Hector, so forget her. She almost hopes Sonya freezes her, because what is there to say, and Birdy realizes that she should freeze her, the way Coach tells them to ignore the other team's trash talk and play the game.

The bell rings, finally, and Mr. Calderon reminds them of their assignment before letting them go. Sonya's closer to the door. Birdy stalls, putting away her things, checking her phone, hoping she'll leave, but she just sits there, letting the rest of the class file out as if waiting to get her alone.

When Birdy stands, she stands.

Sonya walks toward her, digging in her backpack for something. Why does Birdy's mind fix on a poisoned apple? She wants to appeal to Mr. Calderon, but he's busy erasing the board.

Sonya pulls her hand from the backpack and holds out a small black tin Birdy recognizes as the one from the engraved aviator watch she gave Hector for their anniversary, the watch he wears every day. It's just like him that he kept the tin.

It's also like him that he'd send it with an emissary, making it Birdy's responsibility to formally accept it, like a token of surrender. "Thanks."

"Why would you do that to him? I don't understand."

Birdy wants to say she doesn't either, but it's none of Sonya's business. "It wasn't going to work out anyway."

"So you tell him. You don't do this. The worst part is that you run around like you don't even care. Well now you do. It doesn't feel so good when it happens to you, hunh?"

"You don't know anything about it," Birdy says, sensing Mr. Calderon eavesdropping.

"Everybody knows about Myles. All you had to do was ask me, I could have told you. Ask Lydia or Casey Conley. This is what he does, and he always goes back to her. What makes you think you're special?"

"I don't," Birdy says, trying not to act surprised.

"For someone so smart, you're really dumb."

The next class is trickling in, and after a pitying shake of her head, Sonya retreats, leaving Birdy to grapple with this new accusation. It's a lie designed to hurt her, and it has. Lydia and

Casey Conley are both her size, and dark, as if she's just one in a long series of conquests. She zips the tin with the watch into her backpack, wondering what she's supposed to do with it.

In the jostling hallway, the hordes are unavoidable. She ducks her head, following the flow, a parade of faces streaming past, their eyes probing, trying to see inside her. His locker's on the way to trig. Even now, defenseless, racked with doubt, she hopes she might spot him without the girlfriend—a wish so idiotic she has to agree with Sonya. Of course he's not at his locker. She passes it casually, keeping an even look on her face. She turns the last corner before her class, and there by the door is Elena, her ride-or-die, waiting to rescue her.

Birdy tells her what Sonya told her.

"I never heard about Casey Conley," Elena says. "But Lydia, yeah."

"Why didn't you tell me?"

"When was I supposed to tell you? You didn't tell me till two days ago."

"I'm so stupid."

"Stop," Elena says, but now Birdy can't get the idea out of her head. All of their promises, all of their most private moments—everything she thought was special wasn't. She might have been anyone.

In her trig notebook she finds another rose from Friday and can't recall what she was feeling then. As Mrs. Sczerbinski drones on, Birdy methodically boxes it and buries it with crosshatching, finally blacking the whole thing in so she can't see the outline.

In the halls Elena clears the way like a bodyguard. They have the same schedule through lunch and decide to ditch the caf and grab some drive-thru—anything to get off campus. Birdy doesn't feel like eating, but it's a relief not to have to keep up the act. They take Elena's jeep, and as they bomb along Route 1, Birdy lets her face go slack.

They choose the Taco Bell by the Job Lot because it's fast and cheap and Elena loves Baja Blast. Birdy takes a couple bites of her Crunchwrap and closes the box. Elena's still working on hers when her phone dings. She checks it with one hand.

"Oh shit, look at this."

It's a video of Myles's Eclipse, still parked against the fence. The camera pans along the side, showing where someone's keyed it, an unbroken scratch like a road winding through the paint from back to front. They've even done the hood, a big messy X, and though she shouldn't feel any loyalty to Myles at this point, the shittiness of it makes her stomach hurt.

She doesn't think Hector would do this, with his love of cars, but she's not sure of anything anymore. Somehow she'll end up getting blamed for it.

"It wasn't me," she says.

"It's from like two minutes ago."

"You're my witness. I was with you the whole time. Who posted it?"

"Some rando."

Belatedly, Birdy thinks of her own car, an easy target, off at the end of the lot—as if she needed any more drama today.

Though she has only two classes left, one a study hall, she doesn't want to go back.

"Don't quit now," Elena says. "You've almost made it. This is the tough day. It'll get easier from here."

As much as she loves Elena, as they toss their trash and head for Westerly, it feels like a mistake. Things are definitely going to get worse. She still hasn't seen Hector or Myles or the girlfriend face-to-face, and can't avoid them forever. She's afraid the waiting is only a small part of the price she has to pay.

Her car's fine, no scratches or smashed windows, just dirty. His Eclipse is gone, her teammate Monica Chaudhry's Outback taking its place. She scans the rows for Hector's Charger, and wonders if he came in at all. As a kind of penance, she wants to see him as innocent, but who else would have keyed Myles's car—Gregory? They've taken sides. The only thing they agree on is that she's not worth fighting for.

In the halls, she expects the girlfriend to be lurking around every corner, or right outside the door when classes change. The sheer size of her worries Birdy. When she and Josefina would slapbox as kids, she'd always end up red-faced and humiliated. There's no way she can hold off those long arms, and the girlfriend's not Josefina. She's not going to stop when Birdy starts crying.

Study hall and then English, and she's made it through the day. All she has to do is get to her car, and she has Elena by her side. She's prepared for a mob calling her names, but there's no one lying in ambush by her locker, no lookout posted at the smokestack. It's almost disappointing. She knows this won't be over until she faces the girlfriend, and she's ready now. Whatever happens can't be as bad as this waiting.

"I'll call you tonight," Elena says, and Birdy thanks her.

"Come on," Elena says, as if it's nothing. "You my girl."

By reflex, before she gets going, she checks her phone, and then is angry with herself. Dumb, Sonya called her. All the time she thought she was happy, she was being played. Now everyone knows it.

The radio is her enemy, and the CVS, the signs for the airport and the beach, the Walmart with its busy lot, even the liquor store with its cooler full of champagne. The roads, the trees, the sky. Nothing in the world is safe anymore.

At home, her mother treats her like she's sick, making her favorite chicken croquettes for dinner. Birdy picks them apart and scrapes the remains in the trash, hoping she doesn't notice. If her mother's talked to Josefina, she doesn't say. She sits on the couch and knits, endlessly patient, her ball of yarn falling to the floor, spooking Ofelia. The Yankees have the night off, so they watch *Dancing with the Stars*, which normally makes Birdy laugh, but she's tired, and halfway through the second hour she bails, giving her mother a kiss.

"Tomorrow's another day," her mother says, as if that's a good thing.

"It is," Birdy says.

Upstairs, she texts Elena to say she's going to crash and turns off her phone, closing the door on the world, except her mind keeps cycling, flashing on the two of them in the room overlooking the sea, the fire and the cool sheets and his mother's knickknacks—all lost now, present yet forbidden to her, as in a dream. She opens her eyes and is wide awake, the walls tinted red from the power strip under her desk. She punches her pillow and shifts positions, but nothing helps. How do you stop thinking? How do you stop wanting someone?

The next day's no better. Elena tries to help, but Birdy hasn't slept or eaten properly in too long. At school she can't relax, always on high alert. At soccer practice, running wind sprints, she gets dizzy and Coach makes her sit out, further separating her from her teammates. She's so tired she wishes she could quit everything.

She's just changed out of her cleats in the parking lot and gotten into her car when the message pops on her phone. She doesn't know the area code and thinks it's spam, but checks anyway.

Soy Oquendo, it says, and she's saved.

How could she ever doubt him? She's not stupid, she's just not brave.

Soy Oquendo, she answers.

Waiting for him to finish typing, she laughs at her greed, glancing around to see if anyone heard her. Already she wants more.

MU, he says.

MU to

It's a burner phone like drug dealers use, and the secret that keeps her going through the week. Suddenly she's invulnerable. She begins eating again, to her mother's relief, and laughing at the TV. She still can't sleep, but now she has something to hold on to in those empty hours. He's not supposed to be talking with her, he confesses, and though she's risked everything for him and lost, the admission flatters her, because it's all she wants: he can't stop either.

Thursday night she's at work, helping Mr. Futterman and Sandra close up, coming back from the cardboard-only dumpster, when, from out of the darkness, flying at her in full stride, the girlfriend attacks.

Before Birdy can react, she's on her, grabbing her hair, landing punches. Birdy raises her arms to fend her off, but the girlfriend bashes her in the forehead, knocking off her visor. Birdy backpedals, stumbling, her legs tangled. As she goes down, she catches a blow to the root of her ear that sends a bolt of pain branching through her skull. She falls on the concrete and covers up, curling herself into a ball in the shadow of the dumpster. The girlfriend kicks her in the hip, in the ass, in the small of the back, making her grunt, then finally stops and stands over her, panting, faceless.

"That's what you get," she says, pointing. "You fucking remember that."

SOS

The weekend before Halloween was supposed to be our father's, but sometime Thursday he called our mother at the Elms and canceled. He had to work, she told us over dinner, which wasn't unusual. It was the dead time of year between the leaves and the snow, and when he could, he picked up extra money under the table working construction, helping roofing crews button up the new places down along the water before winter set in. We were used to him disappearing on us. In some ways it was a relief. Whenever Angel had to work Saturdays, I'd be left alone with him, the two of us struggling to fill the hours until she returned. In this case, what was unusual was that instead of complaining about our father's unreliability—bailing on us so late—our mother apologized for him, as if, for once, it wasn't his fault.

The only plans the cancellation changed were mine. Fridays our mother and Russ had a standing date, and Angel, suddenly free, announced that she was going to the movies with Myles. To save me from being home alone, my mother decided I should stay over at my grandmother's, a solution that felt to me like a punishment.

"I'm here by myself all the time," I said.

"I know," my mother said. "I don't like it."

"Have fun," Angel said.

"I can watch Brookie but I can't take care of myself."

"It's just for one night," my mother said, because she knew we hated the place. When she and our father first separated, we lived at my grandmother's for a year—Angel and me in the basement, where even now our grandfather's barn coat hung in a cedar closet smelling of mothballs and mouse poop. We were sure the house was haunted, if only by our mother's past. Pictures of her were everywhere, but just from her childhood, as if she'd died in a prom-night car crash. Nothing had changed since she'd moved out, even our grandfather's recliner still faced the old console TV, the Naugahyde on its arms rubbed shiny. Our grandmother didn't have cable or internet service, and her phone looked like a prop from an old movie. Draped over the handle of the oven were calendar tea towels from the 1970s. She lived in the kitchen. She drank instant coffee and smoked Carltons nonstop, her fingers and teeth discolored from it, listening to talk radio all day, absorbing conspiracy theories that leaked out after a few glasses of what she called dago red. She believed Obama was a Muslim, an opinion our mother would goad her into admitting and then ridicule her for, leading to uglier, more personal jabs we wished we could unhear, but she was our only blood besides Aunt Mil, and close by, and if we didn't always get along, she was there for us when no one else was.

"It's not going to kill you," my mother said. "Tomorrow we can have Movie Night, how's that?"

It wasn't a fair negotiation. As the innocent victim, I figured I could make one demand. "And cottage pudding."

"And cottage pudding."

"Okay," I said, in a tone that let her know she still owed me.

"Thank you," she apologized.

Friday I took the bus home with Brookie, walking her to her door and making sure Mrs. Tidwell wasn't watching before crossing the road and slipping behind the Line & Twine. It had become my sanctuary even more than the TV. When the weather was nice, I did my reading for English sitting on the mossy concrete parapet of the dam, watching the smooth black water pull the leaves over. We were reading *To Kill a Mockingbird*, Scout getting assaulted in her ham costume, which I thought was terrifying. Downstream there was a heron that fished the shallows of the far bank, and it had grown used to me, the two of us utterly still, intent on our work.

Inside, exploring the second floor, I'd discovered the accounting office, where my grandmother had kept the books. The floor was covered with yellow and pink invoices other kids had scattered around. The desks had been ransacked, but the contents weren't worth stealing, so there was still a fair number of rusty three-ring binders and moldy file folders and—my prey that Friday—dried-out rubber stamps. I wanted to find one for my grandmother not as a bribe or a peace offering but to disarm her. The Line & Twine meant so much in our family's history that I knew she'd be thrilled to have a memento from it. She was happiest when she was talking about the past, and this would give her the opportunity. I set my backpack on a desk and kicked through the nest of papers until I unearthed one. I was hoping for a stamp that said PAID or OVERDUE, but this just had the date: 11 FEB 89. DUPLICATE, IN, OK—none of them was any better, and I wanted to have some time alone before Angel got home, so I settled for the first one, hoping the date had some significance.

I let myself in with my key, locking the door behind me as my mother had instructed. I hung up my jacket, tossed my backpack on the couch and headed straight for Angel's closet.

Saturday night, when I'd checked on the tank, the bag of balloons had been opened. After a couple tries with the valve, I managed to fill one up. I stood in front of her mirror so I'd get the full effect. The gas felt cold as I breathed it in, and tasted vaguely sweet. I held it in a second, my cheeks puffed out. I'd planned on singing "We are the Lollipop Guild," but before I could start, the room wavered and dimmed.

I lost my grip on the balloon and it flew away, looping the loop.

"Whaaaaa," I said. Instead of squeaky, my voice was deep and slow, like a giant waking up. I was there in my sister's room, seeing everything, but somewhere else too, far away, in my own private audience, watching it all. Her dresser with its matching knobs looked so strange—so serious—that it made me laugh.

The room grew darker, as if there were an eclipse. The girl in the mirror lurched toward me, grinning, arms out like a zombie. Face-first, I ran into the wall and bounced off, toppling backwards, falling against Angel's bed, giggling so hard that I cried.

I don't know how or where Myles got it, but the tank was full of nitrous oxide—laughing gas. I'd never done drugs or been drunk in my life, so I didn't know what had happened, only that I wanted to do it again. I learned to sit back in a chair or lie down on her bed and inhale just a quick pinch so I didn't black out. Since then, I'd returned to her closet every time I was left alone—another reason I wasn't thrilled about going to my grandmother's. Now I wanted a few hits before Angel came home, and crawled toward the dark corner, ducking under her hanging clothes, pushing the milk crate with her roller skates out of the way.

The box was gone.

It had been there yesterday. They could have picked it up at lunch, or maybe they'd cut class. I shouldn't have been surprised. The weekend was party time. I'd just come to rely on the tank being there, a secret within a secret.

Myles dropped Angel off just after five, knowing our mother wouldn't be home before five-thirty. She went upstairs and came down again, looked in the fridge and then sat next to me on the couch, texting.

"What happened to the tank?" I asked casually.

"Don't even," she said, dismissing me with a flick of her hand, not because she was mad, but because she knew it was a bluff. Telling our mother would be a serious breach.

She finished texting and pinned me with a look, as if giving me a chance to retract the question. "You think I don't count the balloons? There weren't that many."

As I tried to muster a defense, she pulled up a picture on her phone and showed it to me: Myles, angelic, passed out on her bed. "You're lucky you didn't kill yourself. And you're supposed to be the smart one. Fuck me."

"I thought it was helium."

"I don't care. Leave my shit alone."

"Okay."

"No 'okay,' because you keep doing it. Next time it'll be something else. It's not cute or funny. I don't do it to you."

I agreed, but thought that was different. I didn't have any secrets worth hiding.

She went back to texting, I went back to watching TV, as if we were good, and we were. Whatever grudges we had, we knew each other.

Our mother was running late and told me to get my things together so she could take me straight to our grandmother's. Though the tank was gone, I still resented being treated like a child, and when she dropped me off I let her know, as evenly as I could, that I was fine staying home by myself.

"I know you are," she said. "I just feel guilty leaving you alone so much lately. It's my problem."

While I was relieved to hear this, the realization had come too late to save me. I was still spending the night at my grandmother's.

She'd been waiting for us. She opened the front door and stood there draped in my grandfather's cardigan with her arms folded and the storm door closed to keep in the heat. My mother didn't get out of the car, just waved and dropped me off as if delivering a hostage. By the time I climbed the porch stairs, she was gone.

"I thought maybe you got a better offer," my grandmother said.

The sweater came to her knees and had two roomy pockets like a smock, one that held her cigarettes and lighter, the other a collection of used tissues. She wore it indoors, three seasons out of four, and though I'd seen her wash it with Woolite in the kitchen sink, when she held me, the reek was overpowering. In her kiss there was a sour hint of wine. I wasn't surprised. It was past five.

"You're looking healthy," she said, which I took to mean fat. Between the cigarettes and the wine, she barely ate. My mother was always bugging her to try the supplements she gave her patients at the Elms. Her skin was gray, her neck wattled.

"So are you," I said.

"I put you in your mother's room, if you want to get rid of that. Are you hungry?"

"Yes," I said, though I wasn't at all, because I could smell something cooking. She had her own schedule, and nothing was going to stop her.

My mother's room still had her furniture from high school, including a red beanbag chair that looked like a smushed tomato. On the dresser, among snapshots of her from that era, stood a framed prom picture, my mother a bombshell with her décolletage, her date shaggy-haired in a baby blue tux. I could never remember his name, though my grandmother brought him up often. She'd been his champion, and never forgave my mother for picking my father. My mother had been an only child, a miracle after a series of miscarriages. Her entire life she'd had to bear all of their hopes, something, as the baby of the family, I was glad I didn't have to do. If it was strange staying in her old room, it was better than the basement with its mice and spiders and Angel shaking the pullout bed with her crying.

For supper, my grandmother had made my favorite, SOS—creamed chipped beef on toast, or, as my grandfather called it, shit on a shingle. We never had it at home because my mother hated it. The cream sauce was rich, the beef salty, the toast underneath softened just enough. It was a dish you had to eat fast or it congealed into glue. I burned my mouth with my first bite, then waited for her to finish her tiny serving before asking for seconds.

"Leave room," she warned, because she'd made Grape-Nut pudding with hard sauce, another favorite normally reserved for holidays. She was catering to me, making me feel bad that I hadn't wanted to come, and to show my appreciation, after I did the dishes and she settled into the recliner to read the paper, I went upstairs and brought down the rubber stamp.

"Oh my Lord," she said. "Those were the days. Every morning we had to change the date. The ink got all over your hands." She opened her arms for a bony hug. "Thank you. That was very thoughtful of you. You're a good girl, Marie. You have a good heart."

From experience, if not by nature, I was wary of sentimentality, and at this point she'd had at least four glasses of wine, so I discounted everything she said.

We watched *Jeopardy!* and *Wheel of Fortune* together, another ritual, my grandmother padding to the kitchen for refills during the commercials, the level in her glass higher than at dinner to save her a trip. For having played these same games for decades, she was surprisingly bad at them. She forgot the categories and flubbed easy questions, sat stumped, muttering to herself, repeating the right answer under her breath the second after a contestant said it, as if she'd known all along. Like my mother, she grew sloppier as the evening wore on, weaving toward the kitchen doorway as if she were on a listing ship, missing her pocket, her lighter dropping to the floor, and I wished I were at home.

When *Wheel of Fortune* was over, she picked up the *Sun* again, absently commenting on the follies of local politicians as if I knew who they were. At least she hadn't started on Obama. I was flopped on the carpet, trying to watch *Ghost Whisperer*, thinking she'd be going to bed soon, when she lowered the paper and, from out of nowhere, doing her best to sound sincere, said she was sorry about my father.

He was a subject I knew better than to discuss with her, and just nodded, hoping that was it.

"You'd think he'd have better sense at his age."

When I looked back at her, she wasn't addressing me but some invisible person standing in the middle of the room, possibly my grandfather. I imagined she talked like this when she was by herself, sharing her never-ending grievances with the dead.

"I shouldn't say anything. Your mother wouldn't like what I have to say, so I'm just not going to say anything. I'm not getting myself in trouble again."

She raised the paper, leaving me frustrated, unable to fight back. She'd ruined *Ghost Whisperer.* Right at nine, when it ended, she rinsed her glass, made me stand and give her a goodnight kiss, and went to bed, hauling herself up the stairs by the railing.

My father, as my mother would have to tell me Saturday night, after cottage pudding, had gotten into a fight outside a bar and was in the hospital. He was fine, he just had some cuts on his face. They were keeping him for observation because they thought he might have a concussion.

I didn't cry, partly because I didn't believe it. By how little she was saying, I knew she wasn't telling me the whole truth. For that I would have to go to my sister.

"Who did he have the fight with?"

"Who do you think?" Angel said.

"Russ," I said.

"No, dummy." Meaning Wes.

"How do you know it was him?"

To me, at thirteen, my sister seemed to move through an underworld of secrets, the hidden currents of desire that ruled life open to her, while deep down even the people I thought I was closest to were unknowable, a complete mystery.

"It was in the paper," she said.

3

Birdy's hip is the worst, bruised purple and black, and so tender it hurts just lifting her leg to step out of the shower. She doesn't remember being hit in the ribs, but the proof's in the mirror, a brown island the size of a fist. She locks her door before getting dressed, confusing Ofelia, lies down on the bed and grits her teeth as she pulls on her jeans. In the bathroom, she does her makeup like any other day. Behind her one ear there's a lump, but besides a slight brush burn on the tip of her chin, which could easily be from soccer, her face is untouched. She was afraid she'd have an egg on her forehead, and thinks it's funny that her visor saved her. She turns her face one way and then the other, dabs a little concealer on her chin. No one will know.

Her mother doesn't, or Birdy wouldn't be going to school. She'd rather stay home with a couple of icepacks, but they're playing Chariho, and he's supposed to meet her after the game. As far as she knows, they're still on. She's not going to let her keep them apart.

She's told no one, not even Elena. She doesn't want to be news. This is between her and Myles, not the whole school. The girlfriend's plan has already backfired. Once he sees what she's done, Birdy's sure he'll choose her.

As she turns into the lot, following the line ahead of her, she's on high alert, checking her mirrors, expecting, any second, the girlfriend to come screeching from between the parked cars, smash her window and drag her out. Instead there's Hector, leaning against the trunk of his Charger, talking with Gregory and Sonya, who bounce when they see Birdy coming.

She's prepared to drive right by him, and is surprised when he waves her down. The way he spoke to her the last time, she thought he was done with her.

He doesn't lean in the window, stands back as if she might drive off.

"What?" she asks.

"Hey. I need that ticket for the dance."

Next Friday's the Halloween Hop. They were supposed to go together, so this means he's taking someone else. That's why he's talking to her.

"I don't have it on me."

"Just whenever."

"Yeah."

"A'ight," he says, in that fake way she hates.

"That's all you want to say?"

"Unless you've got something you want to say."

She's already said she was sorry, that it was her fault. What more does he want—a reason why? Once, she wanted to be with him all the time. When did that change?

"I'll get you the ticket."

"A'ight," he says, letting her go, and she wishes she had a car like his so she could peel out, leave him choking on a cloud of smoke.

She doesn't want to know who he's going with, but Elena tells her anyway: Brianna Mendes.

She's a teammate from spring softball, their second-best pitcher, and though Birdy shouldn't care, she feels betrayed.

"I thought she and Josh were a thing."

"Not for a while."

"She's okay," Birdy says.

She has no right to be hurt, only humiliated. Changing classes, she tries to keep up with Elena and not favor the one leg. As always now, she's sure everyone knows and that no one feels sorry for her. If they knew about the fight, they'd say she's just getting what she deserves, even her friends.

The same on the soccer bus. Traveling to away games, it's a tradition to show off their dance moves in the aisle, but this time when the music starts booming, she stays in her seat—*Got me lookin so crazy right now, your love got me lookin so crazy right now*—watching the ponds and boatyards and strip malls slide by, and none of her teammates calls her name.

In warm-ups, stretching and getting loose, jogging through their possession and keep-away drills, she feels okay, just a little sore, but once the game starts, she can't run at full speed and gets to balls she'd normally corral unchallenged a step too late. Chariho's midfielders are big and physical—horsey white girls the girlfriend's size—and after letting a couple of them push past her, out of frustration Birdy tries a sliding tackle, tripping one, and receives a yellow card. Coach screams and points to his head. It's not a question of thinking. Her whole game is speed. Without it, she's both undersized and slow, easy pickings. Midway through the first half she goes up for a header, but her timing's off. She's coming down just as the Chariho player launches herself, driving her shoulder into Birdy's chin—harder than any punch of the girlfriend's—and lays her out.

Birdy tastes blood and stays down.

"Get up," the other player says, offering a hand as if she's faking.

The ref inspects her and waves over the trainer and Coach, who sit her up. The trainer has her hold her head back and pinches the bridge of her nose. As they walk her off, one by one her teammates file past and pat her shoulder, offering the usual words of encouragement. It's the most they've spoken to her all day.

Their team isn't good, and losing Birdy hurts. They're down 3–0 at the half, and after Coach gives them a pep talk, he takes her aside and asks how she's feeling. He doesn't know anything, he just wants his player back, and she's grateful to be treated like a normal person for a change.

"I'm okay," she says, but a few minutes into the second half her nose lets loose, leaving dark streaks on the bib of her jersey, and the ref stops play and motions her off. She's never quit at anything, yet it's a relief to have an excuse not to run anymore. For the rest of the game she stands on the sideline with an ice-pack, reminding herself that she tried.

The final is 7–0, and the bus ride back is quiet. No one blames her, but she knows when they remember the game, they'll remember not just the lopsided score but her getting hurt, as if the two are related. They might as well be.

It's dark by the time they get back, a trio of spotlights angled up at the flag. As they pull into the lot, she doesn't see his Eclipse. While that was never the plan, she'd let herself daydream that he'd be waiting for her, a sign to the rest of the school that they're together, but after the day she's had, she's not surprised. He hasn't texted. He won't be at the beach. She'll turn around and go home, tell her mother she didn't feel like hanging out after getting injured. At least now she has a reason for the bruises.

All the way down to the shore, she tortures herself. They haven't been together in so long that she's afraid he doesn't want her anymore. This is supposed to be their big reunion, proof they can't stay away from each other. She should be happy, but the fact that they still have to creep around bothers her. It's not a secret. He needs to be honest with the girlfriend, and with her. They can't keep doing this. It's not fair to anyone. If he won't tell her, she will. All this she rehearses as she passes the state beach with its RVs and the Water Wizz and the darkened carousel. She wants him to be shocked by her bruises, wants him to kiss them and tell her he's finished with the girlfriend. It seems so simple to her. She doesn't understand. After everything that's happened, how are they still together?

The house is dark, as she expected, confirming her worst fears, but it's a trick. Even before she turns into the driveway, the garage door slides up, letting out a widening band of light, and there's Myles, ducking under it and coming out to meet her, which he's never done before. Nimble as an acrobat, he crawls onto the hood of her car, clawing at her windshield as she pulls into the empty bay.

"You're such an idiot. What would you do if I drove into the wall?"

"I'd die." He lowers the door and leads her into the bright kitchen. "What happened to your chin?"

"Your girlfriend happened, that's what." She pulls down the waistband of her warm-ups to show him her hip, which looks even worse now, yellow around the edges.

"Whoa. Oh my God."

"She kicked me. She's crazy. She jumped me at work." She lifts her jersey and shows him her ribs.

"She didn't say anything to me."

"Yeah, well, she sucker-punched me and then kicked me when I was on the ground. Maybe you want to ask her about that."

"I'm sorry, that's fucked-up. Are you okay?"

"It hurts."

"I'll bet. Jesus, I'm sorry."

He has champagne out on the counter. As if to change the subject, she takes a glass and waits for him to raise his.

"I missed you," he says.

"I missed you too." She kisses him. "You know this is stupid."

"I know."

"What are we going to do about it?" She lets the challenge hang there in the air between them. "I know what I want."

"I know you do."

She hates it when he goes quiet on her like this, as if she's ruined the mood by making him explain himself. All she wants is for him to be on her side, and he can't even do that.

"I hate this," she says.

"Yeah."

They've reached this same impasse dozens of times, usually over the phone, his silence a kind of surrender. What makes tonight different?

"You're the one who texted me," she says. "I could have kept going. I would have been miserable, but I could have."

"I couldn't. I barely made it this long."

She's flattered, almost glad, knowing he was suffering too, and again, as so often with him, she lets her sympathy outweigh her judgment, setting down her glass and kissing him, closing her eyes and staying there, tasting the champagne, losing herself in the warm slipperiness, dizzy with sensation, until she takes his hand and leads him upstairs.

The room is dark, but there's no time for a fire, no need. They've been apart too much these last few weeks, and pitch into bed, still kissing, tearing at each other's clothes, fumbling with buttons. Finally they're free, meeting each other, skin to skin. She still has her knee socks on, a minor distraction as she bears down on him, concentrating on the warm center spreading, when she feels a space opening somewhere in her head and a fresh flow releasing. Blood, coming from her nose.

"Sorry," she says, pinching the bridge and tipping her head back, too late.

"It's okay," Myles says, trying to keep going, but they've already stopped.

He hits the light to find some tissues for her. While there are bright drops of blood on his bare chest and stomach, there's also what looks like a homemade tattoo, in black marker, just above where they're still joined, of a heart and the girlfriend's initials, clearly in her hand.

"What is that?" Birdy asks, staring, though she knows precisely what it is.

There's no point trying to finish now, and she lifts off of him and covers herself with the sheets, spotted with her blood.

"I think it's supposed to be funny." But he hides it.

"It's not funny. Why didn't you tell me? At least give me a warning. Fuck. I don't understand you two."

"She's afraid of you."

"I'm afraid of her too, but I don't go writing my initials on you. That's crazy."

"She thinks you're trying to steal me, and she's right, you are."

Birdy's not sure if she wants to now. Why is he defending her? That's just as bad as letting her write on him—worse, actually.

"I can't do this again," she says. "You need to figure out what you want."

"I want you."

"Then you know what you have to do."

He ducks his head, rubs his neck. "I do."

"Then do it. I'm going to take a shower."

She wants him to stop her, to hold her, to beg her not to leave. When he doesn't, she sees it as another loss. At least Hector was never weak. When he promised to do something, he did it.

In the bathroom mirror, she looks like she's been beaten. It feels that way, and even the needling spray of the shower doesn't help. Why did she think this would change anything?

Out of habit, or maybe to apologize, he joins her, but in the bright light the writing seems even more obscene, the ink fresher, as if it might rub off on her. An orange pouf that must be his mother's hangs from the shower caddy. Birdy squirts some bodywash on it and holds him from behind, reaching around and scrubbing at the offending letters, scouring his skin till it's pink, as if, with enough effort, she might erase them.

Carol doesn't tell the girls she's going to see him, because they'd want to come too, and he's already screwed up her plans enough. It's Sunday afternoon, her only time to relax. She'd rather be watching the Pats and eating nachos, but instead she says she's going shopping—not entirely a lie—slips what she needs from the medicine cabinet into her bag and heads out. They won't miss her. Angel has work, and Marie's happy to stay home, a luxury Carol wishes she had. She feels like she's always rushing around town, trying to cram in her errands. It's her own fault, as her mother likes to remind her, as if she's alone out of pride.

When they were first married, Frank took care of the cars and the yard and the bills. Now, on his own, he's helpless. They've been divorced eight years, and he still calls to see if he can borrow a thermometer or a hot-water bottle, as if buying his own would be a waste of money, and why bother? As long as she's around there's no need. She used to joke that he only married her because she was a nurse, but it's true, there's always something wrong with him, and she always falls for it. Like today. She could have told him to go to the Urgent Care, but here she is, driving across town to save him fifty bucks.

Sundays the restaurant does dim sum, and she has to park up the block, in front of the sketchy Middle Eastern head shop, the bottom half of its shattered glass door fixed with plywood. The mom-and-pop package store where he cashes his checks is open, and the laundromat where he does his clothes, busy on the weekends. She hates visiting his place because it depresses her. When he moved in, freshly separated from her, she thought it was temporary, the first thing he could find, but it makes sense. Add in the Mobil and its mini-mart across the street, and everything he needs is right here.

She thinks of the Mews, the view from the balcony, and feels guilty, as if she's leaving him behind. Russ has been talking about taking her and the girls to Bermuda for Christmas. She's been meaning to get some guidebooks from the library but doesn't want to jinx it.

His mailbox is one of two at the bottom of a steep staircase, the neighbor's name in both Chinese and English—Chin. She rings the bell and waits with her hand on the knob for him to buzz her in, then shoulders it open. The smell of five-spice fills the stairwell, growing more suffocating as she climbs. Before she reaches the top, the door swings open, letting out the play-by-play of the Pats game, and there's Frank, waving, smiling as if this is a happy occasion, one eyebrow shaved and crusted with blood under a line of butterflies.

She should ask if it hurts, fawn over him, her champion, but she's tired and just tips his face to the light so she can inspect the damage. The skin is split along the top of the socket, an injury she sees all the time at the Elms from falls. "It looks pretty clean."

"I used the stuff they gave me but it's almost gone."

"I brought some you can keep."

Inside, the bareness of the place reminds her of why she hates visiting him, the living room and kitchenette spare as a cell. After their years together as a family, it's hard not to see him as lost. She has him sit on the couch and look up at the ceiling light while she removes the butterflies, dabbing at the tacky adhesive with rubbing alcohol.

"Close your eye."

"I feel bad," he says, "missing their weekend."

"You should have thought of that."

"I wasn't thinking. He was just running his mouth and I got pissed off."

"What are you, in high school?"

He laughs. "In high school I would have kicked his ass."

She doesn't want to know what Wes said. He might not have said anything. Even though Frank has no right, he still gets jealous. Like her mother, when it comes to men, he doesn't trust her judgment.

The charge is assault. The way he says it, he makes it sound like a mistake, as if Wes should have gotten more.

"How much is it going to cost you?"

"I don't know, I've never had one before. Whatever it is, it was worth it."

"Was it?"

"Yes," he says.

"I'll let Marie know you said so."

"I can take them next weekend."

"Next weekend's Halloween. Ange has her big dance."

"What about Marie?"

"Marie's trick-or-treating with Brookie. You can wait another weekend."

"I guess I'll have to."

She cleans the wound with some Betadine from work and gives him the bottle. As she's applying new butterflies, the Patriots score and then on the kickoff recover a fumble.

"It's getting out of hand," he says.

"Shoot. I wanted to watch that."

"Thanks for doing this."

"Yeah," she says, concentrating on the last one, and thinks this is as close as they've been in a long time. He knows she'll always care for him, for the people they used to be. She can't blame him for wanting that back.

"Stay for a beer?"

"No, I should get going. I've got shopping to do."

"I didn't forget your check, it's right here."

"Thanks, I can use it."

He doesn't want to let her go, and after chatting in the doorway for a good ten minutes while the Pats drive the field and score another touchdown, she finally escapes.

"Ay carumba," she says, starting the car.

At the end of the block she makes a left, leaving Pawcatuck, crossing the bridge back into Rhode Island. If she followed the road to the right she could hit McQuade's and do her shopping with all the other mothers, but it's too expensive, and that's not the plan. Instead she stays straight, cruising through Westerly, past the library and the high school and up Granite Street, heading out of town, retracing the route she used to take home from work, waiting for the same lights, pausing at the same stop signs, thinking about how things change, and ends up at the duplex, parking behind Wes's truck so she won't get towed. Climbing the stairs, she thinks she's getting her exercise today.

"You're late," he says, over the game.

"Sorry," she says. "I had to make a house call."

The Yankees are going to the World Series, and her mother wants to throw a party. Between soccer and work and trying to see Myles, Birdy doesn't have the time, but can't say that. Now, for five hours, she'll be trapped in the house with Josefina and

Kelvim and all the aunts and uncles and cousins asking her questions about Hector. They might as well invite him.

Her mother wants to make a huge pot of tripe and bean stew, and fresh *papo secos* to soak up the sauce—her father's favorite, as if he might show up. She's been wearing his hat from when they beat the Mets while she stays up late watching the games. Now she wears it around the house like a talisman, as if to take it off would be bad luck. Birdy understands. When she's going to see Myles, she likes to wear the same red bra she wore their first time, washing it in the sink at night if she has to. Like her mother, she cares too much and has no control over what happens. She'll do anything to keep believing.

What about Shrimp Mozambique for an appetizer? And they have to have fresh cheese to start. Her mother breaks out her tin with her index cards, stained and thumbed soft from a lifetime of use.

"Do you think people are going to want codfish cakes?"

It's already too much food, too much work, but she's excited, and Birdy can't discourage her. Once they have the menu set, Birdy helps put together a shopping list, checking the cupboards to see if they have enough rice and piri piri sauce and tomato paste. She's so focused that for a few minutes she doesn't think of herself and is glad for the distraction. Often now she thinks it would be better if they just stopped. Sometimes she wants to feel nothing. At others that's exactly what she's afraid of.

Game 1 is Wednesday night, meaning she'll have to come straight home from practice instead of detouring down to the beach.

"Yankees suck," Myles says when she tells him, because, like most of her friends, he's a Red Sox fan.

Tuesday they're both working, and Friday's the dance, so they'll see each other only Thursday night. He seems fine with it, which bothers her. She needs him to try harder.

"We could just cut," she says, a jab, because despite all his promises, his days still belong to the girlfriend.

"When's the last time you cut?"

"Senior barbecue."

"That doesn't count."

"I can get out of practice."

"How?"

"I'll just say I'm not feeling great."

"And your coach won't mind?"

Again, she sacrifices her schedule for him. She knows it's pathetic—Elena doesn't have to nag her—but at this point she's beyond pride. She'll give up anything to win him, including herself.

The hard part is telling Coach, who's always liked her. Wednesday at lunch, she stops by his office inside the gym, where he's eating a grinder not from her work, the paper wrapper taking up his blotter. Even if she wasn't lying, she hates asking him for special treatment, and the explanation tumbles out of her. Though he has no reason not to believe her, she almost wants to show him her hip to prove her case.

"That's fine," he says. "Take care of whatever you need to take care of. We're going to need you for North Kingston."

She's getting her way, so why does she feel ashamed? It seems too easy, a cheat, and sitting in class, thinking of the beach, she wonders if there's anyone she won't lie to. Even Myles doesn't know her whole heart.

Leaving the lot, she's paranoid, imagining Coach or the girlfriend is watching to see which way she turns. All the way down 78, she checks her mirrors as if she's being followed.

He's there, waiting for her, his car parked in the driveway rather than hidden in the garage. He gets out as she pulls alongside it, and just from how he waves—closemouthed, a single flip of his hand—she knows something's wrong.

The kiss he gives her is friendly, and when she pulls him closer he holds her off as if they might be seen.

"What's up?" she asks.

"Let's take a walk."

So they're not going inside. She's grown so used to their routine that it's a shock. They only have an hour and a half. Maybe that's what he's thinking.

The sky's blustery, and the beach is empty except for a surfcaster's pickup far down by the breachway. They turn their backs on it and walk toward the sweeping curve of the point with its precarious outermost house, nothing in front of them but gulls and plovers picking through the wrack. As they walk, he looks at his feet, at the waves, at a trawler far out on the horizon, and she knows.

Why now? Why today, when she's just lied so she could be with him? He could have waited till tomorrow at least. She's been preparing herself for this since their first kiss, yet she feels dizzy and nauseous, as if she might fall over or get sick. She wishes he'd take her hand. She has the urge to run, but the sand is soft, and her hip twinges with every step. She shouldn't be here. She should be at practice where nothing can happen.

"I've been thinking," he says.

"That's not good."

"It's not. I don't know." He knows she hates it when he says this, because he does know, he just can't say what he means because he's afraid. He wants her to say it for him.

She stops to make him stop, and he looks at her, a look that says he's sorry, that he hopes she'll forgive him—not now, but maybe eventually. She feels like she's being sentenced, any choice she might have had taken away. It's the girlfriend, she's certain, not him. He's trying to be kind, which only makes it worse. It would be easier if he was heartless. Even now, she wants to believe in him.

"We can't do this anymore," he says, as if he's thinking of both of them.

The terrible thing is that, secretly, she agrees. She's tired, and it would be a relief to quit trying to be someone she isn't. She could go back to being the old Birdy everyone likes, except that Birdy's gone.

"Why did you have to come back?" she asks. "Why couldn't you just let things be?" She hears Hector asking her why and realizes she's become him, and how perfectly that fits. She can just picture Sonya laughing at her.

"I shouldn't have. It's my fault."

"Fuck yes, it's your fault. Jesus, Myles. I left someone for you. Do you understand that? He was a good person and I left him for you."

"I know."

"I can't just go back to him. You don't have to go back to your crazy bitch of a girlfriend because you never left in the first place. I know I'm not the first one either. I'm not even in the top three." None of this has anything to do with the decision. She just needs him to feel bad.

"You're the only one that meant anything."

"Fuck you," Birdy says, pushing him away, and wheels and heads for the house.

"That's why I came back," Myles calls after her. "For you."

She keeps on, limping across the uneven sand, aware that he's trailing her. She doesn't want to cry, but the wind's in her face, and her vision blurs, her nose runs so she has to wipe it with the back of her hand.

"Stop," he says, catching up, but still doesn't touch her.

"You're an asshole."

"I know I am. I fucked up everything. That's what I don't want to do anymore."

"What happened? Yesterday everything was fine."

She's being cruel, making him explain, when it's clear to her, and has been all along. There were moments when she felt that he was hers, but only when they were alone.

"I don't know," he starts.

"Stop fucking saying that. You know. Just be honest with me for once."

"I've been honest with you the whole time. That's why this is so hard."

"It's not that hard," she says. "You've already decided, obviously."

It's true, because it silences him. They trudge along, the surf foaming in, then receding, endless. On a clear day they could see Block Island, but with the clouds there's nothing but a dark line. After watching the planes and the ferries how many times, they never made it there.

"It might not work," he says, "but I have to try."

"Is that supposed to make me feel better?"

"I'm tired of lying."

"Then tell her the truth."

He looks at her helplessly, as if she's being unfair. Because this is the truth. He's telling her.

They're almost to the house now, angling away from the water through a gap in the dunes where the seagrass rustles in the breeze. She thinks of her mother kneading the dough for her rolls, the stew already bubbling on the stove, and wishes she were there.

"And I blew off practice for this."

It's supposed to be a joke, but he can't stop apologizing. Even if he's sincere, she's tired of it. To ice him, she checks her phone and sees her mother's been trying to call her. She needs paprika.

How quickly she turns cold, as if she doesn't know him anymore—as if, with one word, they're enemies. His stupid piece of shit car, she's glad Hector fucked it up.

"Do you want to come in?" he asks.

"No, I don't want to come in. What are we going to do, play video games? I'm going home. I've got shit to do."

As she's unlocking her car, he comes closer as if he wants to kiss her, but she holds up a hand. "Really, dude?"

As her last words to him, they don't seem momentous enough. Following traffic up 78, the radio off as a precaution, she thinks of what she should have said, something cutting and romantic, but can't hold on to her thoughts. She's hurt and angry and free, replaying their conversation, zeroing in on exactly where he's wrong about them, and why, as if when she gets home she'll call him and continue the argument, breaking down his assumptions one by one until he agrees with her. What does she hope to win? She can see them strolling along the beach like actors on a bare stage, and understands why he couldn't let her inside. She wonders if he's done it before, if she's just another girl he took for a walk when he was finished with her.

"I came back for you," he said. Why did that surprise her? Even now, she can't think of a reason why he'd risk everything a second time—and after the girlfriend posted their picture. She remembers seeing *Soy Oquendo* on her phone and feeling rescued. So why, after coming back, didn't he fight for her? That seems worse than not coming back at all. It's impossible to make sense of, but her mind tries, in line at the Stop & Shop, and driving along the river as dusk falls, and well after she gets home and feeds Ofelia and helps set up the buffet on the dining room table.

Her mother's at the stove in her apron and her father's Yankees cap, humming and happy. The stew is simmering, the *papo secos* laid out on baking sheets so she can pop them in at the last second.

"What time is everybody coming?"

"I told them seven."

"What time does the game start?"

"Eight."

Birdy loads a cooler with beer and ice and opens the red wine, sets out Diet Coke for Josefina and club soda for Tia Miranda and Sprite and Orangina for the kids. Olives, pretzels, beer nuts, crackers for the fresh cheese—everything's ready, and she slips upstairs to change, Ofelia at her heels. She needs to stop checking her phone, and leaves it plugged in beside her bed. She wishes she could just go to sleep. Everyone's going to want to talk about Hector, the whole party dissecting their breakup like they know anything about it, like the people at school or on Facebook. They think they know her, but they don't anymore, even her mother. For a little while, Myles did, at least she hopes so. Otherwise what was it all for?

She changes into her father's old Jeter T-shirt, thin and soft from washing, so big it hangs to her knees. "Your turn." She tugs her own Jeter T-shirt over Ofelia's head, shoves her paws through the armholes. "Look, we're twins," she says, but Ofelia isn't happy, rubbing her shoulder along the side of the bed, trying to pull it off.

The doorbell rings, and Ofelia bolts downstairs, barking like it's the mailman.

It's Tio Luis and Tia Eva, always the first to arrive, bearing a bottle of champagne for when the Yankees win the series.

"We'll drink it together," her mother says.

"I like the shirts," Tio Luis says.

Her mother has to watch her codfish cakes, leaving Birdy to take care of their guests.

"What can I do?" Tia Eva says.

"Nothing," Birdy says, and steers them into the dining room, where the wine is.

Behind her the front door opens, and Ofelia charges.

"I'm not afraid of you," Josefina says, Kelvim right behind her with Luz in her carrier. She takes Birdy in her arms, holding her an extra second, and Birdy thinks of Myles, how on the beach he wouldn't touch her. It's another mystery. Whatever bound them together wasn't strong enough.

Josefina hangs on to her arm, looking her up and down. "You look good, *irmãzinha.* We'll talk later."

Luz is the star, pudgy-cheeked and toothless, all gums and drool and fat fingers. Her mother takes her from Kelvim and sways back and forth, dances with her, cooing in her ear, puts her father's cap on her head, boops the tip of her nose so she laughs, and Birdy's happy to fade into the background, helping Kelvim take their baby gear up to Josefina's old room.

"Sorry about you and Hector," Kelvim says, dumping it in a heap on the bed.

"Yeah, thanks."

"I heard he quit his job."

Who cares? she wants to say. At the same time, she wants to know what it means. "He had that job forever."

"You're still at D'Angelo's."

"Yeah, I wish I could quit."

"Anyway," Kelvim says, and Birdy remembers how Hector always saw him as a role model, the responsible young father. Kelvim's the one person he'd be talking to if he was here, and she feels strange, as if she's broken them up too. What hasn't she ruined?

Downstairs, more people are pouring in, Ofelia barking nonstop.

"You're going to go upstairs and you're not going to like it," Birdy warns her, and then, when she doesn't listen, takes her by the collar and hauls her off. "You can come down when you're done being a jerk."

It's time to eat, and her mother needs her help with the *papo secos*, Birdy replenishing the buffet with fresh ones straight from the oven. She waves with her oven mitt at Tia Claudia and Tio Euclides and their three boys waiting in line, at Tia Lucinda and Tia Elvira and her cousins Inês and Paulina and Gloria. The crush is like one of their family picnics, except they're all jammed into the living room, gathered around the one TV. By the time Birdy finishes in the kitchen and fixes herself a plate, Michelle Obama is walking out to the mound with a soldier just back from Iraq who throws a strike to Jeter.

"That's right," Birdy says, turning to show everyone his name on the back of her shirt.

Another soldier sings the anthem. It's drizzling, and the people in the stands look cold. The *papo secos* are light and fluffy, and she sops up the salty stew, watching the Phillies do nothing. Tio Fausto offers her a seat but she waves him off. She's working.

As the Yankees are coming up to bat, her cousin Marco drops part of a codfish cake on the floor.

"Where's the dog?" Tia Hilaria calls, and Birdy realizes she's still upstairs. She waits until Jeter strikes out to release her.

With her door closed, Birdy gets down on her knees and holds Ofelia's face in her hands so they're nose-to-nose. "You need to be good." When she lets go of her, Ofelia romps around like it's a game. "Or not."

They're on the stairs when from below comes a groan that can only be bad news. Birdy hurries down to catch the replay. The Phillies have hit a home run.

"It's all right," her mother says. "It's just one."

The next inning Jeter doubles but A-Rod strikes out for a second time, and the room goes quiet.

"I hate that guy," Tia Eva says.

Nothing's happening in the game, and Birdy leaves Ofelia getting belly rubs from the nieces and helps Josefina clean up the kitchen, soaking the stew pot, putting away the leftovers. As usual, her mother's made too much. They're going to be eating *feijoada* for the next month.

"I'll take some," Josefina says. "It was good."

"It was."

They're alone at the sink, washing and drying side by side, a ritual from girlhood. Birdy expects her to say something about Hector, about how she's disappointed in her. The suspense is a kind of torture she doesn't have the patience for today.

"Kelvim said Hector quit his job."

"Shit, I'm sorry," Josefina says. "I told him not to say anything."

"Why? He likes Hector."

"Everybody likes Hector," Josefina says. "I like Hector. I don't love him. But I don't have to."

Birdy isn't sure what she means, and waits for more.

"You have to," Josefina says.

"I don't."

"I never thought so. I mean, he's fine. What about this other guy?"

Birdy had hoped she didn't know, but isn't surprised. Everyone's on Facebook. "I thought I did."

"So it's over."

"I think so."

"So where are you now?"

"Nowhere," Birdy says.

"Would you go back?"

"To which one?"

"Oh *querida*, I'm sorry." She takes her in her arms, and again Birdy sees Myles on the beach.

"I want to but I can't."

"Don't," Josefina says, holding her. "It doesn't work."

"How do you know?"

"I know, okay?"

"Thank you," Birdy says, because she's grateful for her. They're sisters, bound by blood, by secrets.

They're just composing themselves again when her mother comes in with Luz. "I think people are ready for dessert."

They're having sweet rice, the top crisscrossed with lines of cinnamon in a diamond pattern. Her mother does it freehand, making it look easy, but she's been doing it her whole life.

As Birdy's taking plates out to the dining room, the Phillies hit another home run.

"You gotta be kidding me," Tio Luis says, because it's the same guy.

"It's only two," her mother says, but it's already the sixth inning.

Things don't get better. Besides Jeter, the Yankees can't figure out the Phillies' pitcher. It's a school night, and once dessert's done, people start leaving.

"You're going to miss the big comeback," her mother jokes, kissing Kelvim and Josefina and pinching Luz's cheeks.

It's raining in the Bronx, and when the Yankee reliever gives up two runs, the crowd clears out. Two more runs and even Tio Luis and Tia Eva say their goodbyes. In the end, it's just her mother on the couch watching A-Rod strike out while Birdy puts the chairs back where they belong. After the last out, her mother turns off the TV and helps.

"Thank you," her mother says, locking up, turning off the outside lights.

"Sorry about the game."

"It's just the first game. It was good to see everyone."

Birdy wishes she had her mother's optimism and common sense. It *was* good to see everyone, especially Josefina, but she feels like she's been losing all day and just wants it to end.

Upstairs, there's one message on her phone, and the wild hope it inspires angers her. He can't do this to her again. She can't.

It's Hector, bugging her about the ticket.

She claps the phone down on her nightstand and sits on the edge of her bed, deciding whether she should just tear up the ticket or conveniently forget it, then plucks it from the frame of her mirror and sticks it in her purse.

Brushing her teeth, she's still irritated, and when she gets into bed and turns out the light, there's no way she can sleep. She wonders if Myles is, or if he's thinking of her. She lies there, replaying their talk on the beach, sees the wind whipping his dark hair as they stroll toward the far-off house on the point with its grand chimneys and widow's walk, never getting any closer. Why didn't she fight him harder?

From the darkness at the foot of her bed comes a hacking—Ofelia choking on something. She hitches, then snorts in like a boar, frightening Birdy, as if she can't breathe.

"Hang on." She's going to barf. It always happens when there's a party. She's a beggar, the kids can't resist her, and before Birdy can throw off her covers and drag her into the bathroom where it's easier to clean up, with a wet cough she retches, stretching her neck, her throat opening, splashing vomit on the carpet.

"Perfect," Birdy says.

Friday night is Cabbage Night, and Marie wants to pull a prank, but on who? Angel's at her dance and her mother's off at the casino with Russ, so she's home alone, eating fish sticks and French fries in front of the TV, dreaming up mischief—soaping the windows of Mr. DeRosa's Mercedes or pegging eggs at Mrs. Capuano's front door. Tomorrow she's taking Brookie trick-or-treating, which Marie knows she's too old for, though she still lusts after the free candy, and Sunday Halloween will be over, so it has to be tonight.

The problem is that no one lives on their road. She's explored the abandoned houses around them, but despite their broken windows and smashed sinks and holes punched in the drywall, she's never been tempted to vandalize them, and the mill is her haven, off-limits. She's not interested in destruction but revenge. For that, she needs a target, and one close by. She could sneak down the road through the overgrown backyards and ding-dong ditch Mrs. Tidwell for never paying her, except, like her mother, she feels sorry for her. Plus it's not the same without a flaming bag of dog shit, and where is she going to find dog shit? Technically, she supposes, she could use her own. If she wanted to walk two miles in the dark, she could TP her grandmother's Japanese maple, but that seems like a lot of work, and her grandmother would have to hire someone to clean it up. It's easier to watch *Ghost Whisperer* and imagine doing these heroic deeds, but eventually *Ghost Whisperer* ends and Marie has to make a decision.

As always when faced with boredom, she visits the fridge. Her mother has stashed their candy in the freezer, asking Marie not to eat it all, since Angel would never do anything like that. Marie thinks she's been good, tearing a rodent-sized hole in the corner of just one bag. Halloween's tomorrow, and no one's going to be trick-or-treating on their road anyway, so she fishes out a fun-size Snickers and shoves the whole thing in her mouth and stands there chewing with the door open, another habit of hers her mother discourages. After a second Snickers, she pulls out the big bottle of her mother's wine, checks the level, pops the cork, and with both hands tips it to her lips.

The wine is cold and sour, erasing the taste of gluey nougat for just a second before it returns, even sweeter. She takes another pull, swishing it between her teeth. By itself, it's too tart, and she coughs and makes a face and corks it again. How does her mother drink a whole bottle? Marie puts it back exactly as it was, the label facing out, and grabs another Snickers to get the taste out of her mouth.

Upstairs she opens her mother's top dresser drawer and inspects the new arrivals her mother has picked out for Wes or Russ or whoever she's trying to impress this week. Black, red, leopard print, strapless, underwire, push-up, bikini, French cut, even a thong Marie doesn't want to picture on her. Does she wear the same ones for both? Because that would be gross. And how much did they all cost? Her own bras are the color of Band-Aids, her underwear bought in packs of six at Walmart.

She pulls off her shirt and chooses a zebra-print right on top with stiff cups, modeling it in the mirror. Her mother's always complaining that her boobs are too big. Now Marie has to agree. Her own look puny inside the giant cups, which hold their shape all by themselves. In the mirror, with her belly hanging out, she looks like the sexless blob she is, and she turns her back and gets dressed, vowing to never do this again, knowing she can't resist.

In Angel's room she's more careful, aware there may be traps. Her dresser holds no secrets, or her nightstand—places a burglar or little sister would search first. She goes straight to her closet, checking the floor in the corner before starting on the wall of shoeboxes, opening them one by one, reaching into each shoe to make sure there's nothing shoved up in the toe.

She's patient—Angel's always hiding something—but in the end all she finds is a stone pipe and a butane torch she's seen before. She unzips the cedar-smelling storage bag and goes through the pockets of her winter coats, but there's nothing. She stands, fists on hips, staring at Angel's hanging clothes and the rug and the milk crate with her roller skates.

It's in the first skate she tries, deep in the toe—a Motorola flip phone she immediately opens. The voicemail is empty, a disappointment, and the messages. There are no recent calls, as if the phone's been wiped clean, but the battery's only half charged. Her first thought, from thousands of hours of TV, is that Angel's dealing drugs, a secret too explosive to use as leverage. Marie turns off the phone, shoves it back in the toe of the skate and heads downstairs again, wondering what she can do with this new information.

She hits the fridge for another Snickers and more wine, stops at the front window and looks out at her mother's car in the drive. She could call her mother and tell her Wes is outside and drunk and wants to fight Russ, but her mother wouldn't think it was funny. What can she do and not get in trouble? She's thinking of her father as a potential victim when, across the road, against the long, unbroken wall of the Line & Twine, three shadows materialize—three boys dressed in black hoodies like ninjas.

They stop and drop their backpacks. They're a tagging crew, two of them waving spray cans in wide arcs over their heads, throwing up graffiti while the third serves as a lookout. She steps away from the curtains so he won't see her. In the dark it's impossible to tell what they're writing, it's only when a car comes and they drop to the ground that she can glimpse the rounded outlines of words. Just their nicknames, she expects, like the other drawings on the wall, but the idea of them doing it like a commando raid makes it exciting. She watches them to see if the third guy will get a chance to put something up, and is thrilled when he does and is faster than the other two, blasting with both hands. When he's done, they gather their cans and vanish into the night again, and she wishes she were going with them.

In her room, in imitation, she changes into all black, even her socks. They use bodywash, so the only bar soap she can find is a grimy block of Ivory by the basement work sink. As she climbs the stairs, she hides it at her hip like a gun. She turns off the hall light and the porch light and waits a minute for her eyes to adjust before slipping outside.

The road's empty, the moon low, almost full, its pale glow casting shadows. The wind rises, rattling the bare branches, and Marie creeps down the stairs and crouches in the well of darkness between the house and her mother's car, listening. On the far side of the Line & Twine, the river purls over the dam, invisible. Nothing's coming, but she waits, patient as an assassin, the sharp-smelling soap moist in her warm hand. No one can see her hunched by the front tire, and she likes the feeling. Just by being outside in the night, she's dangerous, a predator.

An engine growls in the distance, slowly growing closer. She bends lower, her head almost touching the ground, and peeks beneath the car. Down by the Tidwells', a pair of headlights appears. For an instant she's afraid it might be Angel and Myles, bailing on the dance to make out in her room, but the engine sounds deeper, maybe a pickup truck. If it's Wes, she's not sure what she'll do.

Run. As it closes the distance, accelerating down the straightaway, its lights reach beneath her mother's car as if they're trying to find her, and she sits up and hides behind the front tire, her back pressed against the fender, one with the darkness. The light flares brighter, its reflection turning her side of the car and even the weeds on the driveway visible, a geometry of shadows sliding across the porch and the front door, then disappearing as the truck roars past. Marie laughs. She wants to do it again.

She could savor the feeling of almost being caught all night, but it's cold and she's not wearing a jacket, and after a line of three cars passes, right into one coming the other way, she's done. The wind rises and falls. The river purls. She kneels and peeks over the hood. No one's coming, yet she steals around the back hatch of the car like a cat burglar, keeping low. With a corner of the soap, in giant letters across the rear window so it can be seen from the road, she writes: WHORE.

The cruel satisfaction of it—the truth—is too much, and undoes her. If she believes this, she's not ruthless enough to tell the rest of the world. It's not a prank, and before anyone can come along and see it, she x'es out the letters, turning the word into an abstract pattern, obliterating that with overlapping circles, building up a smeary tornado of soap, moving on to the side windows only when she's confident it says nothing.

On their way to the dance, both of them in costume, pleasantly buzzed from pregaming with Jäger at Ryan's, Myles confesses that she texted him today.

"I thought you'd want to know."

He drops this bomb while he's driving, barely glancing at her, as if it's minor. In his grinning Joker makeup and green fright wig, he could just be fucking with her, but he's serious. This time, he wants Angel to know, it's really over. After lying to her for so long, he wants credit for being honest.

"I didn't answer her."

Why does he do this to her? He must like seeing her lose her mind. Yesterday she held him as he cried, apologizing for ruining things again. Now she feels like hitting him.

"When did she text you?" she asks, to see how long he's kept it secret from her.

"Right before work."

Like a stalker, the little bitch knows his whole schedule. Angel will have to check his other phone for the exact time—probably the only reason he's telling her now.

"You didn't text her."

"Definitely not."

She leaves this alone so he can hear how guilty he sounds. "She doesn't learn."

She holds out her hand for his phone, which he offers without a word. As part of her Poison Ivy costume, she's wearing pointy green nails, and has trouble pressing the buttons.

"Where is it?"

"I deleted it."

"Next time don't delete it. I want to see it."

"Okay, I won't."

He's her ally now, her accomplice, as if to make up for the unforgivable. The awful thing is that she wants to believe him. They've been together so long that when he confessed, she was terrified of losing him. Now he's come back to her, penitent, their bond even stronger. What happens when he goes away to school is a question she can't answer, but until the day he leaves Ashaway, for better or worse, he's hers.

At school there's a police car by the entrance—empty, they realize when they pass it. The cop's inside, providing security, standing behind the table where two mothers in red Thing 1 and Thing 2 shirts and blue beehive wigs are taking tickets.

"I love the color," Mom 2 says of her fiery copper hair.

"Manic Panic." She's put some effort into her look, especially the knee boots, and is glad someone noticed besides the creeps (including the cop) peeking at her cleavage.

The dance is in the cafeteria, the insistent plinking of John Carpenter's *Halloween* theme reaching them, the DJ exhorting everyone to give it up for Michael Myers. In the hall, beyond the trophy case, a photographer has erected a black backdrop, shooting keepsake portraits of the couples before they ruin their costumes. The line is long. Angel recognizes the little bitch's ex near the front with Brianna Mendes, the two of them dressed like Indiana Jones and Karen Allen, and sees that Myles has too, standing up straighter, puffing out his chest. He still hasn't fixed his car, which, like everything else, she considers his own fault.

"Don't even think of it," she says.

"I'm not going to start anything."

"No, you're not, so stop."

The bouncy bass line of *Ghostbusters* winds up, irresistible, making people move. *If there's something strange in your neighborhood.* They could skip the line, but she's told Myles she wants a picture of them—one more condition of his surrender—and is relieved when Hector and Brianna take their turn and go straight in. She almost wants to leave but can't. She's on a mission to show everyone they're still together, Hector the opposite, which seems easier to her. Though she knows it on the most basic level, she doesn't want to examine too closely what they have in common, afraid of feeling sympathy for him. It's simpler to think of him as an enemy.

"Hey, losers," Mikayla waves, flitting by, wearing the same Britney Spears outfit she had on at Ryan's the other night, showing off her midriff. They've been mistaken for sisters in the past. It must be the discovery of the text, because as Myles watches her go, for an instant Angel's jealous of even her.

Ryan and Lindsay show up as Fred and Wilma Flintstone, wearing slippers that look like bare feet. For their tribe of friends, the dance is just an intermission before the after-party. There's nothing to drink here, no place to smoke, and the music is lame. By the end of the night they'll be gathered around a bonfire like always, Myles playing for the crowd but singing to her.

"This is a rip-off," Ryan says, so loud the photographer can hear. "Take your own damn picture."

"You don't have to buy it if you don't like it," Angel says.

"You hear about Casey Daigle? She's fucking knocked up." He clucks his tongue.

"That's crazy," Angel says.

"That's why she and Benny broke up," Lindsay says.

"Wow," Myles says when they're gone. He's always surprised by what other people do, as if he's completely innocent.

"You know, they talk about us like that," she says.

"No they don't."

"They feel sorry for me and think you're an asshole."

"I don't know if I'm an asshole," he says, weighing the word. "Maybe a dick."

"A nice dick who can be an asshole." She kisses his cheek, leaving a violet imprint of lipstick on his white makeup.

"That's fair."

It feels good to joke about it, as if it's ancient history, unable to touch them, but it only takes someone's phone dinging to turn her thoughts sour, and by the time they make it to the front of the line, she knows what she has to do. She told the bitch what she'd get.

The photographer's in costume too, wearing a fedora with a press pass sticking out of the band, using a boxy old camera like something from the movies.

"The Joker I know," he says, escorting them to the backdrop. "And you are . . ."

"Dr. Pamela Isley. Poison Ivy. Uma Thurman in the movie."

"Didn't see it, but I love the nails." He takes away the stool. "I'm going to have you stand because we want to see your costumes. Oh, I like that. Keep your head just like that. Now, can you look at him? Boyfriend and girlfriend?"

"Yes," they say at the same time, making them both smile.

"That's good. Chin up. Now, if you can put your left hand on his waist."

The spotlights are hot, and as they go through the ridiculous poses, looking into each other's eyes, trying not to laugh, she feels both exposed and closer to him. She hopes everyone in her class passing by sees them. It would be too much if she kissed him (and against the dumb rules), but she pictures it, an open declaration to the whole school. This will have to do.

"All right," the photographer says. "Let's do one in character."

That's easy, since she's practiced in the mirror at home. She squares off, curling her hands into claws, sneers like Uma Thurman and glares at the camera as if ready to do battle. Beside her, thumbs hooked in his vest, Myles throws his head back and crows a silent, maniacal laugh. Of all the shots, it's the one they like best, the one they absolutely have to have—two supervillains joining forces to defeat their nemesis.

Her mother feels bad that she has to work on Halloween, but Birdy says it's all right, the weather's crappy and she has nothing better to do. What does another lie matter? She called in sick Thursday, unable to stomach the idea of being there, or anywhere with people, really. She sat in the parking lot of the state beach while the sun set, texting him, waiting for him to answer, then kicked along the surf in the dark, watched by the empty houses and closed hotels, imagining a hurricane scouring everything clean.

Now that he wants to see her again, she can laugh at how melodramatic she was being, recalling the details so she can embroider her story for him, her sadness proof of her love. After this last breakup, she thinks he's as helpless as she is. Why else put each other through this? It's a comfort, despite all of their mistakes, to know they're the same.

It's cold and drizzling as she follows the road through Ashaway, past the Liquor Depot, where Hector no longer works, the lot full of anonymous cars, past the Mobil and the Bi-Lo and Crandall Field with its picnic pavilion and play fort, past the post office and the old mill running along the river—scenery she's come to associate with him, with the anticipation of being loved, even the granite works and its headstones, the Lucky House Chinese restaurant, the used-car lot where the cops sometimes sit. In its homely familiarity, it's all magical to her, charged with a fleeting beauty, like the leaves.

The sky's dark, the day waning. As she joins 78, as if someone's flipped a switch, the streetlights ahead of her flicker on, silver, showing her the way. Everything is a sign, the world teeming with meaning. A mile later she misses the light at the Post Road and has to sit there facing the CVS where the girlfriend works, a warning she tries to ignore. She doesn't want revenge—today she can't be bitter—and yet, after everything that's happened, she can't deny the outcome has a certain sweetness. How resilient love is, how surprising.

The light drops to green and she leaves the CVS behind, cruising by the Stop & Shop and alongside the airport, one eye out for cops, since it's the last day of the month. She doesn't stop to change at the tennis courts with their dank women's room, just keeps going, turning onto Winnapaug Road and climbing the final hill, the meadows and salt ponds spreading before her, and in the distance, instead of the dark line of the ocean, a white wall of fog.

A mist has blown ashore, hanging thick as smoke over the rental cottages and motels, turning everything ghostly. It's like driving through a cloud, the double yellow line floating out of the murk. She tries her high beams, but they only make it worse. She knows the way, and still she has to crawl along, finding the stop sign and the clock that's always wrong.

At the state beach she can't see across the lot, and takes advantage of the cover to change into the red top he likes, tossing her uniform into the backseat. She fixes her hair and chews a last piece of gum, ditching it while it's still juicy to redo her lipstick. Maybe it's the makeup, or all the weight she's lost from not eating, but in the mirror she looks different, her face sharper, more defined, and she turns her head side to side to appreciate her new cheekbones, gives herself a knowing smile. This is what love does.

Leaving the lot, she has to wait for a car to pass, its foglights cutting tunnels through the soup. It's only as the marked SUV crosses in front of her that she sees it's the police, which makes sense. Who else would be out in this?

If a part of her thinks she's being desperate—or stupid, as Elena would say—running back to him every time he changes his mind, she'll try anything rather than feel the way she did last night, Cinderella missing the ball.

She slips past the midway attractions by the Water Wizz, a single spotlight outlining the carousel pavilion, where, years ago, in a much-rewound video, her father sat her on a painted horse, steadying her with a hand on her back as they circled, and she thinks of her mother. The Yankees are playing game 3 tonight. When Birdy gets home, she'll be in front of the set, her bursts of cheering scaring Ofelia. Her father's been gone so long. How does her mother do it? A few days without Myles and Birdy's a wreck.

The mist billows over the road, pushed by the sea breeze. The rain's coming down harder now. Here, on both sides, are the houses she'll never own, gray-shingled cottages decorated with lobster buoys and weathervanes, fences made of old surfboards. It's taking longer than she wants, but she can't go any faster. There are no storm drains here, so close to the ocean, and water's ponding on the shoulder, taking up half the lane. She straddles the yellow line to skirt the puddles, has to slow when the road's covered, inching through, her tires pushing a wave ahead of her like a ship. The cop is long gone. She imagines stalling and having to call Triple A, how she'd explain it to her mother. She'll save it for Myles. He'll laugh when she tells him the story, rewarding her courage with a kiss.

The light ahead belongs to the Breachway Market, meaning the beach club is next and then the bridge where she and Josefina went crabbing as kids. She's late, but she's going to make it. Now she's afraid he won't be there, that he's left a message on her phone saying he's had to cancel. Their plans are so flimsy. Even when everything goes right, she doesn't believe in them.

From the outside of the house it's impossible to tell if anyone's there. The windows are dark, the driveway empty, rain spattering in the gravel. Her headlights sweep across the porch. Normally he opens the garage door before she can stop. She's right, he's blown her off, and then, as she reaches for her phone, the door glides up and there are his feet, and him, ducking under the lip and waving her into the empty bay.

Instead of coming around to her side, he waits by the kitchen door.

"It's bad out there," she says.

"I know, it just rolled in."

He seems tentative, which she blames on the breakup. He probably thinks she's angry. Is she that hard to read? After the last time, she needs him to wrap his arms around her, but the garage door senses something and won't close, retracting with a clatter so he has to hit the button again. They both watch it go, hoping. This time it stays down.

"I'm glad you could come," he says, almost formally, as if he's asked her to a meeting, and instead of kissing her, opens the door to the kitchen, letting her go ahead of him. She expects to see champagne waiting for her, and is disappointed to find the counter empty, only a roll of paper towels and a bottle of hand soap by the sink.

He puts the chain on the door, and before she can register it as strange, as if on cue, from the living room comes the girlfriend, smirking.

Birdy's first instinct is to run, but it's futile. The door's locked, and Myles already has her from behind.

Lanoxall

Growing up in a small town, you learn to keep your secrets, otherwise you'll never live them down. At thirteen, the product of alcoholics, I'd had lots of practice. I knew my mother would never find out who soaped her windows.

"I can't believe this," she said when Russ dropped her off. "And you didn't hear anything?"

I told her about the tagging crew, pointing to the proof on the Line & Twine. It was Cabbage Night, there were roving bands of boys everywhere, every car a target.

"This is when I miss having a garage," she said, though we hadn't had one in forever.

I said I'd help. We didn't have a hose, so she had to fill a bucket and lug it outside. Cold water was no good. The soap was so thick in places, we needed hot water to dissolve it. Steam rose from our sponges as we scrubbed, foamy clusters of bubbles sliding down the windows.

"At least it's getting a bath," she said, and thanked me when we were done as if I'd restored her faith in teenagers.

Later, while I was reading on my bed, daydreaming of the trades I was going to make with Brookie for Butterfingers, Angel came in and closed the door.

"It was from the basement."

"What?"

"The soap you used. It's like half the size it was."

It wasn't—I'd been careful, rubbing dirt into the corners so it would look old—but I didn't think I could deny it with a straight face. "So what?"

"So someone might like to know about it."

"Someone might like to know about a phone."

I thought we were joking, but she shot her arm out and clamped a hand around the back of my neck and jammed my face into the bedspread, leaning her full weight on me, holding me down. "Someone's supposed to keep her nose out of my shit."

On her way out she slammed the door, knocking my bathrobe off its hook, making my mother yell from downstairs: "Don't slam the door!"

Even something little like this, she couldn't let me win, and I hated her, and hated myself for being weak. Halloween was my favorite holiday, and she'd ruined it. If she tried to apologize, I'd ask her why she had to be so mean to me, but she didn't, and after Myles came and took her away, I tended my anger alone in my room, ignoring *To Kill a Mockingbird* and imagining all the scathing things I should have said.

We ate early so I could start trick-or-treating with Brookie while it was still light out. Among the million other things her mother was afraid of was Brookie being hit by a car in the dark. Over her bright white Imperial Stormtrooper costume, she wore a reflective vest like a highway worker. It was raining, so instead of a blaster rifle, she held an umbrella. I'd wanted to be a ham like Scout, but my father would have had to help me build the frame, and I settled for being a witch. The plan was for Mrs. Tidwell to leave us off in the middle of town where the houses were closer together and pick us up at the library when the fire siren blew at eight, meaning we had two hours to fill our pillowcases. Like every Halloween, I'd drawn a map tracing the most efficient route, though by now I'd memorized it. I didn't show Mrs. Tidwell the map, because she would have seen that we had to cross Route 3 four times, including twice at the intersection of High Street, where Alex Hanley had been hit on his bike in the middle of the day. Since then the town had put in a crosswalk, but no one stopped for it, so maybe it was good that Brookie was wearing her vest.

With the rain, we didn't have much competition. We were older than everyone else, though knowing it was Brookie behind the mask, no one said anything. In two hours we should have been able to complete the route easily, except she was so slow. We had no problems crossing the street, but she couldn't see to go up or down stairs, and I had to guide her as if she was blind, her umbrella knocking my witch's hat cockeyed, dripping water down my neck. It was cold and I was soaked. Just past the cemetery, not even halfway home, she stopped and said, "I have to go," forcing us to detour to my grandmother's, where I helped her out of her costume and stood by, staring at the bamboo-patterned wallpaper while she peed.

"I should have warned you," Mrs. Tidwell said, like it was funny. "The sound of the rain makes her tinkle."

The haul was my smallest ever, and included two popcorn balls, a twist-tied baggie of loose candy corn and an Almond Joy, all of which I'd end up throwing away. I was so discouraged that I didn't bother trying to trade with Brookie, just rode quietly in the backseat while Mrs. Tidwell quizzed her on all the cool costumes she'd seen. When they dropped me off, Mrs. Tidwell thanked me as if I'd done her a huge favor, and I said it was no problem, but once they pulled away, I let my face drop and hung my head as I climbed the porch steps.

My mother thanked me too, making hot chocolate to warm me up. It had been quiet there, and we had tons of candy left. "Did you and Brookie have fun?"

I told her about stopping at my grandmother's, which she thought was smart of me. In her eyes, I would always be the good one. Sharing the afghan with her, half watching *Scream*, I wanted to tell her I was the one who'd soaped her windows. Instead, I made popcorn and gave her my Milky Ways. To salvage the day, I was hoping to make up with Angel, but by the time Myles brought her back, it was past midnight and I was asleep. In the morning, we went to church, and when we confessed and passed the Peace, I let go of everything and embraced her, vowing, as always, to start fresh again.

Monday night, the lead story on the news was Beatriz Alves. "The Westerly High School senior," they called her, and showed her mother at a microphone in their driveway, holding up her picture. The whole family was putting up flyers. With her doe eyes and heart-shaped face, she looked like Jessica Alba. Though we were the same height, I weighed thirty pounds more than her.

"Do you know her?" my mother asked.

"Everyone knows her," Angel said. "She's on the soccer team."

"That's my worst nightmare, something happening to one of you."

"Which one?" I asked, but neither of them thought it was funny.

Since she was last seen leaving for work, the police were searching for her car. They showed her license plate number like we might memorize it, then cut to a shooting in East Providence.

She was on every night that week, the search following her route to work, which happened to go by our house. Friday, the police set up their mobile command post in the fenced-off parking lot of the Line & Twine, their radios squawking, bringing in dogs and ATVs and a helicopter that hovered low over the river all weekend, scanning the woods and marshes for body heat.

Like anything on TV, the case seemed to belong to another world, even though it was happening right across the road. I knew that stretch of the river better than anyone, and imagined finding her, limp and pale as a fish, caught on the lip of the dam, and telling my story to a reporter. Every night they gave us another clue, as if it was a game. When she'd left home, her mother said she was wearing her uniform, but her boss said she wasn't scheduled to work. She'd recently broken up with her longtime boyfriend, who police considered a person of interest.

"It's probably him," my mother said, with no evidence.

By then Angel had stopped watching, retreating to her room before the news came on, as if disgusted with us playing amateur detective. Volleyball season was starting, and she had practice twice a week, on top of work and seeing Myles, so she wasn't home much. She was popular and busy, and we were used to her disappearing.

Everything after that happened too fast. Because I was in middle school, I could only guess at what led to Myles being questioned, though once it made the *Sun*, I looked up the pictures on Facebook—taken down but still available as screenshots if you followed the links in the comments. Out of loyalty, or because I couldn't believe it myself, I didn't tell my mother. I thought I was in the middle, caught between them, but as usual, I was way behind, keeping a secret they were keeping from me. Angel had already told her, so none of us was surprised when the police called. The question was whether she needed a lawyer, prompting a family meeting at my grandmother's I wasn't invited to, where they decided it might look suspicious. As a fan of Atticus Finch, my answer would have been yes.

The night before Angel's interview, after we'd all gone upstairs and brushed our teeth, my mother came into my room.

She sat on the edge of my bed and held my hands, rubbing them with her thumbs. "You don't know anything about this, do you?"

"No," I said, and thought of the phone in Angel's skate.

"You're sure? Anything. If you do, you need to tell me."

I didn't know if it was still there or not. Either way, it wasn't my secret to tell. "Are they going to arrest her?"

"They're just going to ask her some questions. I'll be there the whole time."

What kind of questions? I wanted to ask, but I'd seen enough TV to know. The idea that she could be involved was ridiculous, though I understood the connection. My mother said it was all Myles's fault, and I agreed with her, but Myles hadn't been arrested. What could Angel tell them that he couldn't?

The next morning I took the bus to school like it was a regular day, while Angel and my mother drove downtown to the police department. When I got home, my grandmother's car was there, and Angel was in her room.

"They didn't talk to her very long," my mother said. "Which is good."

"And she didn't need a lawyer?" my grandmother said.

"She did fine," my mother said.

They didn't want to discuss anything specific in front of me, and when I grabbed my backpack to head upstairs, my mother said, "Leave her alone."

I couldn't. Even on a normal day, her closed door was a provocation. I set down my backpack and crept toward her room, trying to be quiet so they wouldn't hear me downstairs. I put my ear to her door, expecting to hear her crying or whispering into her phone. Instead, she was singing along to Paramore on her iPod, the song from the *Twilight* movie, humming when she didn't know the words, her volume all over the place. *You're always taking sides, but you won't take away my pride.* It was so normal that it was strange, and I backed away as if I'd caught her doing something wrong.

At dinner she seemed the same to me, joking about missing practice, complaining that she had to work Saturday. Maybe she was just relieved. My mother wasn't going to bring up the interview, and I felt that I shouldn't, despite wanting to know everything. I waited until she was back in her room, doing homework.

"How was it?" I asked from the doorway.

She had to think before she answered. "It wasn't bad."

"What did they ask you?"

"All kinds of stuff."

"Stuff about Myles."

"And other people at school."

She was telling the truth and she was lying at the same time, minimizing, the way I lied to my mother about my eating, the way my mother lied to me when she didn't think something was my business, like her drinking, or my father. We were all good at covering things up. I wondered if Angel had lied to the police, either for herself or for Myles. I wondered if she had to, and if they knew.

The next morning I rang the Tidwells' bell to walk Brookie to our stop. Usually she'd be waiting on the other side of the door, dressed and ready to go, her Pikachu lunch box in hand, but this time I had to stand on the porch a while, watching cars fly by. When Mrs. Tidwell finally answered, she opened the door just a crack.

"You go ahead, Marie. I'm driving her today, thanks."

"Okay," I said. She was a grown-up, and I didn't think to ask for an explanation. Maybe Brookie had a doctor's appointment or something.

Like all the houses across from the Line & Twine, theirs was a copy of ours, and as I turned at the end of the walk, Brookie was waving to me from the living room window. I waved back.

At the end of the day, in line for the bus, I didn't see her anywhere. Normally one of the special ed teachers would make sure she got on, but there was no one.

The next morning Mrs. Tidwell thanked me for coming by but said she was going to drive Brookie again. Brookie waved from the window and I waved back. Again, at the end of the day, she didn't show up, and I rode home alone.

When my mother got home from work, I told her. She said she'd call Mrs. Tidwell and find out what was going on. She did it upstairs, where I couldn't hear her. When she came down, she had me turn off the TV and sat on the couch with me.

From now on, Mrs. Tidwell was going to drive Brookie, so I didn't need to go over there anymore.

"I'm sorry," my mother said, "I think it's really shitty of her," and finally I understood that Mrs. Tidwell didn't want Brookie to be seen with me.

I was humiliated and pissed off—not because she'd snubbed me but because she'd been so nice doing it that I hadn't realized. Now I wished I'd soaped her car instead of my mother's.

Twice a day I had to walk past their place. I couldn't blame Brookie, so every morning I'd wave to her like we were still friends, until one day the drapes were closed. I waved anyway, in case she could see me. Sometimes, trying to shame Mrs. Tidwell, I'd wave both arms over my head like I was flagging down a train, but after a while I stopped and passed by the house without looking, as if I didn't know who lived there.

It wasn't the last time we'd be victims of gossip, but at least I was aware of it now. When I climbed on the bus or walked into my homeroom, I wondered how many people knew who my sister was and what she'd supposedly done. I liked school. I was smart and quiet, and if I didn't have many friends, teachers liked me. I was used to my classmates ignoring me, at worst thinking of me as a nerd or a tubbo. Now I'd become something else I had no control over, and dreaded going.

I was just hoping to make it to Thanksgiving break, but that Monday a nor'easter blew in, snapping tree limbs and knocking out power, dumping a record eight inches of rain. The river rose, running high and wild, white water overtopping dams, dislodging a sunken oil drum from its resting place on the bottom and washing it bobbing downstream, past farms and golf courses and abandoned mills and sagging three-deckers, wallowing under the Amtrak trestle and a dozen other bridges as it floated through Westerly, headed seaward. An Avondale man walking his beagle on Graves Neck found it washed ashore and called the police after the dog wouldn't leave it alone. Inside they found Birdy Alves. On the news, they showed the drum, empty now, tagged as evidence. Stenciled on its side, military-style, was the brand name of the original contents, a long-banned chemical used in the mills to soften cotton—Lanoxall.

"Never heard of it," my mother said.

Sitting there beside her, I said nothing, afraid of giving myself away. Because I had, and I knew exactly where I'd seen the name before.

4

Seven a.m., they show up with no warning, banging on the door as Carol's making eggs for the girls, pounding so loud she's afraid they'll break it down. "Westerly Police! We have a search warrant!"

Wes said this might happen, but it's still frightening. The whites aren't set yet, the top layer runny. She turns off the burner, moves the pan to a cool one and fits a lid on it, thinking, by some miracle, she might save them.

A fist thumps the door, insistent. "Westerly Police! We have a search warrant!" It's like a script.

"I'm coming!" she shouts. Why don't they just ring the bell? Men, they're doing it to intimidate her, and she's annoyed that it's working.

Marie has stopped halfway down the stairs to see what's happening, and Carol points at her to go back up. "Tell your sister the police are here."

"She's in the shower."

"Tell her to get out and get dressed. Now."

The fist thumps.

"Hang on!" Carol says, slapping her side of the door, and pretends to fuss with the lock, buying Angel some time.

She expects a big show—detectives in suits, a couple cruisers, maybe a mobile forensics lab, at the least a white van—but when she opens the door, it's just two uniformed officers, a man and a woman, their car pulled into the drive behind hers. The man's in front, with a blond buzz cut and fingerless gloves. He holds a clipboard as if he's taking a survey. In her scrubs and slippers, she feels at a disadvantage.

"Morning, ma'am," he says, as if he wasn't just hammering at her door.

"Good morning, officer."

"Is this 47 River Road?"

"Yes it is." She's smiling, being overly polite, almost mocking him, but can't stop herself, the muscles of her face beyond her control. There's a reason they're here, and she's afraid.

"Is this the residence of Angel Lynn Oliviera?"

"Yes."

Behind him, his partner is drawing on the same blue latex gloves Carol uses at work when she's called on to perform a messy procedure. It makes sense, having a female cop search her room. Though neither has made a move to enter, Carol fills the doorway, blocking it. She knows she's supposed to cooperate, but right or wrong, she'll defend her daughter against anyone who comes after her.

"Do you have any questions before we begin our search?"

"May I see it?" As a nurse, she's an expert at paperwork and is prepared to object to the smallest clerical error, a missing signature or date left blank.

He holds up the clipboard as if he doesn't trust her, making her lean forward, squinting to read the fine print. She's disappointed but not surprised to see that everything's filled out, the issuing judge's signature duly witnessed by a clerk of the court. The warrant authorizes them to search the premises for potential evidence including the suspect's clothing and personal possessions, as well as a specific wish list—her cellphone, laptop or home computer, and any electronic evidence stored therein. Carol thinks it's unfair. Angel's phone is her brain. The police digging around in it is like them reading her mind, rewinding her memory. Though she denies everything, Carol can imagine a transcript of texts from Myles, and wonders if they already have his phone. Myles has never seemed very bright to her, and what she's read online hasn't raised her opinion. She can see things going wrong and Myles panicking. It would be like him to think he could get away with it, not caring that he's made Angel an accomplice.

"Is it all right if we come in?" the man asks, as if it's ever been her choice, and Carol has to stand aside.

The female officer is carrying a sheaf of clear plastic bags. "Can you show us where her room is?"

Do they want her to search it for them too, deliver her daughter to them on a platter?

The girls haven't come down, and when she leads the officers upstairs, both the bathroom door and Marie's are closed. From the bathroom comes the whine of the blow-dryer.

"It's this one."

"Thank you." The man assures her they'll give her a receipt for anything they take, as if she's worried about that, while the woman does a quick scan of the room.

"Does your daughter have a bag she normally carries?"

"You mean a purse?"

"Purse, bag, backpack."

"Yes." It's so obvious. There's no reason she'd have it in the bathroom with her.

"We need to see it."

Carol knocks on the door, and the blow-dryer stops. "What?"

"They need to see your purse."

"And her phone," the woman says.

"And your phone."

Angel opens the door a crack and shoves her purse through, then bangs it shut. A traitor, Carol hands the purse to the woman, who takes it into Angel's room and dumps the contents on her bed. She picks up the phone, turns it off and seals it in a plastic bag.

"We're going to need her to come out of there," the man says.

Why? Carol wants to ask, but doesn't, unsure of her rights. She wishes they had a lawyer, even if her mother has to pay for one.

"They need you to come out, honey."

"Why?"

"It's for our safety and yours," the man says. "I need both of you to hang out downstairs while we're doing our search."

Carol explains that her younger daughter is in her room.

"I need all of you downstairs now, please."

She has to knock on Marie's door and coax her out, taking her hand. Angel flushes the toilet before emerging—a needless provocation, Carol thinks.

The woman leaves off pawing through the tubes of lip gloss and balled tissues and old fortune cookie slips to interrogate Angel. "Is there anything in your room you want to tell us about? Weapons, drugs, anything you're not supposed to have?"

Angel looks at her as if she's stupid, a face Carol knows well.

"I'm giving you a chance to help yourself here."

"No," Angel says.

"They're not going to find anything," she says downstairs, brimming with contempt, but Carol isn't so sure. Sitting on the couch with her arm around Marie, pretending to watch the news as the cops clomp around above them, she thinks she needs to call Myles's parents.

"What am I supposed to do without a phone?" Angel says, like any teenager.

"We'll get you another phone."

"All my stuff's on that one."

How long does it take to search a room? And what are they actually looking for? Angel, Marie, her—they're all going to be late, and rather than wait to be released, Carol gets up and dumps the hardened eggs in the garbage, wipes out the pan and makes another batch, and toast, the three of them sitting down to breakfast together, which they never do. Marie's said nothing since the police arrived, and Carol's relieved to see her clean her plate. Angel picks at hers, as always, but doesn't have to be asked to clear the table. If she's playing the victim, Carol thinks, she also knows they're only here because of her. Because of Myles. Everything goes back to him, and she wonders if right now they're searching his house. She hopes so, but can't say it out loud.

They're taking so long that Marie has to use the basement toilet to pee, braving the spiders. Carol's on her second cup of coffee when the man clumps down the stairs, carrying Angel's laptop and phone in separate bags.

"Are there any other devices she has access to?"

Carol's own phone and laptop, but they've already taken enough. "No, that's it."

"No BlackBerrys, no gaming consoles?"

"Are you almost done?"

"Almost. Just have to write it up."

The woman comes down with two big bags full of clothes, including several pairs of jeans. Carol wants to stop her but watches from the front hall as she loads them into the trunk of the car, the man making notes on his clipboard.

When the woman comes back in, she stops at the coatrack, eyeing the hanging jackets like a shopper. "Which ones are hers?"

You figure it out, Carol's tempted to say, but hands them over.

"It's cold out," Angel protests. "What am I supposed to wear?"

"You can wear one of mine."

"I don't want to wear one of yours."

The woman points to Angel's feet. "We're going to need those shoes."

Fuming, Angel tears them off, dashing them to the floor, and stomps upstairs. Carol expects the woman to go after her, to order her to come down, but she just adds the shoes to the bag of jackets and takes it out to the car.

On the couch, Marie is hugging her knees.

"It's okay, Mimi," Carol says, trying to calm herself as well. They didn't have to do it this way, with all of them there, and again she thinks they need a lawyer, no matter what it costs. "You want to go up to your room? You can."

"No," Marie says, and Carol holds her, vowing from now on to protect her from all of this.

Along with the phone and the laptop and the clothes and shoes, the final inventory the man leaves includes several items she didn't see them take, and several she doesn't recognize, the most surprising a fake Rhode Island driver's license and four bound notebooks they're calling her journal. She's not sure how these eluded her, unlike the pipes and rolling papers and butane torch. She almost wants to ask the cops where they found them, and would if she wasn't so angry and embarrassed. She shouldn't compare herself to them, trained professionals, but she's a mother. Part of her job is searching out her child's favorite hiding places, learning her deepest secrets. She's been too busy, too caught up in Russ and Wes and trying to figure out the rest of her life to understand what was going on with Angel and Myles and this other girl. Now that it's too late, she has a list to remind her of everything she doesn't know.

They should run away. She doesn't care where—New Zealand, Fiji. It's not realistic, but she doesn't see the point of waking up every day and going to school. Nothing they can do will change anything. They're just waiting.

Their parents have agreed it's best if they don't see each other. In the morning, instead of him picking her up, she has to walk to the bus stop like she's in middle school. The days are growing shorter, and it's still dark out, the streetlights buzzing. She stands in the cold as cars swish past, a few honking at her. They used to do it because she was pretty and alone, a menacing catcall that was supposed to be a compliment. She hates it even more now.

The police have impounded his Eclipse, and he's driving his brother's hand-me-down Volvo wagon, tomato-red and so old it has a cassette deck. She's always surprised to see it, as if she's forgotten why. It's so unlike him—such a fitting punishment—that it makes her laugh. They need these little in-jokes. It's just the two of them now.

Today he's right on time, and she ducks inside, glad to be out of the cold, giving him a kiss as he pulls away. The police have sealed the beach house, and Galilee holds too many memories. She needs to be alone with him, but there's nowhere to go, and they're probably being followed. They're supposed to act like everything's normal, which means they can't do anything they'd normally do, as if showing up for class instead of losing themselves in each other proves they're innocent.

"Hear about Casey Daigle?" Myles asks, glancing over, and she can tell it's big news.

"No." Because no one talks to her anymore.

"She's getting back with Benny."

"Shut up."

"She's gonna have it."

"Shut up shut up."

"She's gonna have it and they're gonna get married."

"Whaaat? Where are you hearing this?"

"Ryan." So, Lindsay, who she misses.

"Wow. Didn't see that coming."

"I didn't either."

"Good for them," she says, and she means it. At this point she's so desperate that any happy ending moves her, and as they cross under 78 and head into Westerly, she thinks, crazily, that they should get married. Before she can tick off all the reasons it's a terrible idea, she surprises herself by saying it out loud.

"That's what my dad said," Myles says, like it wasn't helpful. "Then we wouldn't have to testify against each other."

"That's not what I mean."

"No, yeah," he says. "Definitely, we could."

It's obvious he hasn't thought of it, and she shrugs and pretends she wasn't serious. "It's just a thought I had."

"It's a good thought."

"No, it's stupid. I'm not marrying some guy who drives a Volvo wagon."

"Volvo sport wagon," he corrects her, and like that they're back to a safe equilibrium. It takes so little to knock her off balance. A stray thought and she's in quicksand. She tries to think of what happened as an accident, as if she was just defending herself. She didn't mean for it to go that far, she just wanted to scare her off. Now she's sorry but she can't tell anyone, and neither of them wants to talk about it. It's done, and there's nothing left to say.

They do the drive-thru at Dunkin' Donuts and sit in the lot, sipping coffee and watching the time, making sure they arrive at school a few minutes late so the halls are clear. He walks her to class like a bodyguard, but he can't always be with her. Last week one of the girl's friends snuck up behind her during a change and sucker-punched her. She was a foot shorter than Angel, and swung wildly, lunging, trying to knock her out. Her fist glanced off the side of her head, the momentum sending the girl stumbling into oncoming traffic. Angel hunched, covering up, more stunned than hurt, and turned to find the girl on the floor, swearing in Portuguese and spitting at her. Everyone stood back, making space for them to fight. She could have stomped the girl if she wanted—no one would have stopped her—but picked up her purse and kept going. She wouldn't give her the satisfaction of rubbing the spot, though later there was a lump. Since then she's been more careful, but every time the bell rings, she's ready to protect herself. Mikayla walks with her, but none of her other teammates.

In class she doesn't speak unless the teacher asks her a question. Maybe it's her imagination, but she feels like they're picking on her. She takes pages of notes, following along, but often she's wrong, or has to say "I don't know," drawing mocking laughter, because she's not paying attention. Her mind is on Fiji, on the beach, on what's going to become of them. The margins of her notebooks are full of desert islands and sunsets.

In study hall she finds a quiet corner, pulls out the big book and prepares for the SATs, trying to memorize words she'll never use again. The test is already paid for. It's too late for a refund, her mother constantly reminds her. She's not just stupid but thoughtless, not worth the registration fee.

For lunch, they escape, decompressing, comparing their days so far. They drive across the state line into Stonington, where no one knows them, eating fried clams and drinking coffee cabinets, impostors playing at being carefree teens. They have to be back in an hour, so they need to stay close, but what if they kept going, across the bridge at Mystic and down along the shore? There are ferries that run from New London, trains from New Haven. By the time her mother gets home to make dinner, they could be in New York City, lost on a different kind of island. They drain their cabinets, set the plastic tray on top of the garbage can and get back in the car.

At school they find a spot away from everyone at the bottom of the overflow lot and make out before parting again. They only have three periods to go, yet they take so long. Sometimes at night she wakes up and her phone says it's four or five, and she remembers fighting with the girl on the kitchen floor and knows she won't get back to sleep. That's how the afternoon feels, the final hours drawn out, all her patience gone, leaving her mind prey to unwanted thoughts, and then when she's finished, no matter how she lingers after her last class, they have to walk the gauntlet to the parking lot.

Here, after surviving another day of shame, is their reward. Between the end of school and when Marie's bus drops her off, they have forty-five minutes to themselves. It's not long enough to go anywhere, and the police are always watching, so they have to be careful. They stay in Ashaway, leaving his car behind their church. Below the cemetery, hidden in a thicket, there's a pond where her grandfather took her fishing. Even with the leaves down, no one can see them. It's cold, and the old army blanket Myles keeps in his car is itchy, the ground beneath them lumpy, but she doesn't care. There is nothing more than this. Lying there revived, free for a moment, she admires how the trees defy gravity, reaching for the sky. It's not quite winter yet. What will they do when it snows? Eventually the pond will freeze and be taken over by skaters, and they'll have to find a place inside. By then who knows where they'll be—not Fiji. For now it's enough to feel close to him again, if only for this short time. Climbing the hill toward the steeple, she remembers that for all of her sins, she believes in something.

Home, she tries to hold on to the feeling, but it leaks away. Marie's too quiet, doing her homework and watching TV instead of pestering her with a million questions, and she worries that she's afraid of her. While it's silly—she loves Marie—she knows how out of control she's been lately and feels guilty. As if to apologize, she bakes Toll House cookies, serving them hot and still soft from the cooling rack, delivering Marie a stack on a paper napkin and a glass of milk, a bribe she can't resist.

"Who's your favorite sister?" she asks.

Her mother isn't won over so easily, dragging home late, harassed and unhappy, freaked out about dinner. She hangs her purse and jacket on the coatrack and goes straight to the kitchen in her scrubs as if it's a race, telling them she doesn't have time to make the chicken thighs she'd planned on because she forgot to defrost them. She hopes frozen ravioli's okay.

"It's going to have to be, because that's all I've got. Unless *you* want to make something besides cookies. I see someone left me a present." Meaning the cookie sheets.

"I'm going to do those."

"I'm going to need the sink," her mother says, as if Angel doesn't get it.

Everything Angel does makes more work for her mother. Her whole life her mother's made her feel this way. She's always fought against it. Now, with the trouble she's in, she has to agree. How many times does she have to say she's sorry?

Her mother thinks they need a lawyer, as if that will solve all their problems. After dinner, while Marie watches TV, she changes into her sweatpants and slippers and drinks her wine at the kitchen table, doing research on her laptop, sighing and muttering to herself. Angel wants to tell her not to bother, that nothing will help, but lets her believe a good one could make a difference. It's strange. At the same time she wishes her mother would give up, she needs her to believe she's innocent.

Her mother blames Myles, which isn't the same. She thinks he's a spoiled rich kid, with his *Legend of Zelda* tattoos and his fast and furious Eclipse, and stupid for cheating on her. On the phone with her grandmother, she calls him an idiot and a druggie, and Angel wants to defend him.

"I can't believe she's gotten herself mixed up in something like this," her mother says, not quite an exoneration—and totally wrong, from where Angel stands—but it's enough. If she told her mother the truth, she wouldn't believe it anyway. Angel doesn't. Sometimes she sees it happening, like something on TV, not a memory at all, except she knows.

Once Marie goes to bed, her mother feels free to speak openly, swearing at Myles's parents, at the police, at her father. "He's no goddamn help. He can't even pay his own lawyer."

She's only sharing this because she has Angel there for an audience. This should be Angel's cue to leave, but to show she appreciates everything her mother's done, she waits, ignoring the TV, absorbing her complaints about Russ and her grandmother and the doctors at work until it's time for the news, which her mother always watches. Angel can't, afraid she may see the girl's mother, pleading for someone to come forward, and kisses her goodnight, catching a boozy whiff of breath.

"We'll get through this," her mother says, whatever that means.

"I know." It's easiest to agree with her. She won't remember tomorrow anyway.

In bed she texts Myles. Her new phone is cheap and she misses her old one. It vibrates, lighting up, and it's him, singing to her, his guitar strumming softly in the background. *Sundowns are golden, then fade away. If I never do nothin', I'll get you back some day.*

"You've already got me," she says.

"Forever?"

"Forever."

It's how they say good night now, how they say goodbye, not knowing if this might be the last time. Tomorrow they'll do it all over again, sleepwalking through school, driving around town like it's a regular day, following the path down to the pond. In the dark, watching the shadows cast by a passing car slide across the ceiling, she tells herself it's more than most people have, but in the morning she knows it's a lie. They have so little left. They should run away before they lose everything.

That afternoon, having braved another day at school, they're walking up from the pond in the cold, holding hands, when the police step out of the trees, guns drawn. After waiting so long, she's relieved. Her first thought is that she's glad they're together.

"Show me your hands!" the officer in charge says.

They look at each other, ready, finally, but neither of them wants to let go.

Marie's not allowed to see her, for now. There are too many reporters staking out the jail, waiting to ambush them. "I'm hoping things will die down after the arraignment," her mother says. Marie thinks it's a weak excuse until one night she sees her mother on the news, trying to hide her face with her folder full of notes. Though Marie can't say it, the camera makes her look old.

"They're assholes," her mother says. "They stand in your way so it looks like you're trying to run from them when you're just trying to get by."

Every day after work her mother visits Angel for an hour, and Marie feels left out. She can't be home alone, so after school, instead of taking the bus, she walks the five blocks to her grandmother's, imagining the neighbors watching from behind their blinds. She does her homework on the floor in front of the TV, then helps her grandmother get dinner ready. Her mother's never had time to teach her how to cook, and she learns how to make pan gravy and jonnycakes and cranberry bread, her grandmother standing at her shoulder, reeking of cigarettes. At dinner, her mother's impressed, but only for a moment before going on about Angel's latest problem.

"It's crazy how expensive everything is in jail."

"What do they have to spend money on?" her grandmother says. "I thought they got everything for free."

"Toothpaste, shampoo—everything costs extra. Guess how much cigarettes are."

Marie clears the table and does the dishes. The sooner she finishes, the sooner they can go home, where she can watch *Gossip Girl* in peace.

They never remember to leave a light on in the morning, so the house is always dark when they get back. Among the hundreds of crank calls they've received, they've had several from men threatening to rape them. Marie's afraid that one night a man will show up with a knife. She hates waiting on the porch while her mother fumbles with her keys.

Inside, there are a dozen messages on the machine, including the usual obscene tirades and hang-ups and polite inquiries by the *Sun*. Her mother listens for a second, then erases them. If she isn't going to change their number, Marie thinks, why doesn't she just unplug it?

Everyone hates them, as if they're equally guilty of murder. People even call her grandmother and go off on her. The case is all over the news. ANGEL OF DEATH, the *ProJo* calls her. Part of it is how pretty she is. The TV stations use the picture of her and Myles from junior prom where she looks like Amanda Seyfried with her bare shoulders and loose curls. Her mother says it's unfair. Marie, who's envied Angel her whole life, understands there's a cruel justice to it. The ugly want to see the beautiful suffer.

At night the house is quiet with just the two of them, which Marie likes. There's no shouting because there's nothing to fight about. Her mother works on her computer, doing research, tapping the keys. She's serious, and drinking less. The goal is to have Angel home for Christmas. She doesn't talk about the facts of the case, only nailing down a lawyer and bailing her out, as if her guilt or innocence doesn't matter, while Marie tries to piece together the crime like a detective. The *Sun* says the two of them lured the girl to an unknown location where they beat her, then moved the body, putting it in the drum. Her car hasn't been found, a detail Marie thinks is key. She imagines being called to testify at the trial and having to tell them about the barrels in the Line & Twine and the flip phone, but no one's asked. She's the nerdy little sister, too clueless to know anything useful.

She can picture Angel hitting the girl in anger, but not killing her. She's never seen Myles pissed off, but she's observed him with Angel. He'd do it for her. A lot of guys would. She sees it all the time on *Dateline*, the jealous girlfriend who makes her lover kill the other woman. There's no way to prove her theory, no one to share it with, so it never becomes real, remains yet another guilty secret Marie carries.

Ten is her bedtime. She kisses her mother goodnight and goes up. Angel's door is closed but not locked. As she brushes her teeth, she opens it and wanders around her room, not snooping, just taking in the pictures on the walls and her perfumes on her dresser and her textbooks on her desk. Her mother's cleaned and straightened. Everything's artificially neat, awaiting her return. Marie can't believe it hasn't even been a week. It feels longer.

In bed she thinks of Angel in her cell, lying awake on her bunk like Tom Robinson before the trial, except it's different. Once, when they were living at her grandmother's, Marie chipped one of her good teacups while she was washing the dishes and tried to hide it behind the others at the back of the hutch. For days she waited to be caught, and wished she'd confessed. She never did, but it was a relief when her grandmother finally found out, her punishment freeing. Maybe that's what Angel's waiting for.

Her father thinks it's all Myles's fault, like her grandmother, the two of them unlikely allies. Saturday he has Marie for the afternoon, and they climb in his truck and drive to a farm in North Stonington to pick out a Christmas tree, tramping through the rows with a saw. Normally her mother would insist on getting their tree without his help, but she doesn't have time, and she wants the house to be decorated for Angel when she comes home.

"I don't think she really cares," her father says, "but you know your mother."

He's been to see Angel and says she's okay.

"What's it like in jail?" Marie asks, because he was just in it. His eyebrow still hasn't grown back.

"It's not bad. It's boring. And I was only there for a few hours. She'll be all right. She's tough."

"Mom won't let me go see her."

"I think that's probably smart right now."

"I miss her."

"We all do, Mimi. We're going to get her out of there. It's just going to take a while."

"You know what I want for Christmas?"

"What?"

"Her."

"Yeah. I hear you. We're working on it. What else do you want?"

"Nothing," she says, and though he tries to wheedle something concrete out of her, she doesn't buckle.

"That's what you're going to get then, a whole lot of nothing."

He must tell her mother, because Monday when she gets back from visiting, she says she's arranged for Angel to call them tomorrow night. It's expensive, so they won't be able to talk long, and everything they say will be recorded, so they'll need to be careful not to discuss the case, but both Marie and her grandmother will get to speak with her.

"Merry Christmas," her mother says, and Marie's too happy to say that's not what she asked for.

On the way home she's thinking of everything she wants to say to Angel. It's been so long since she's had something good to look forward to. It *is* like Christmas, the gift a surprise. She wants to call her father and thank him for listening to her.

"Thank you," she says.

"For what?" her mother says.

"For my present."

"It's just a phone call. Let's not make it a big thing. I don't want you to be disappointed."

"I won't be."

"Sometimes you do that, you know, build things up. I just want you to keep a lid on your expectations, okay?"

"Okay," Marie says, hard, to stop her from ruining the moment, so they're both sunk in silence when they pull into the driveway and see that the front window has a hole in it.

"Goddammit," her mother says, and jumps out, leaving the lights on.

The hole is the size of a basketball, and jagged, cracks radiating to the frame, as if any second the rest of the glass will fall out.

Her mother calls the police before making sure the front door's locked.

"Fuckers," she says, trying to find the key, and it isn't clear who she means.

Inside, it's freezing, and there's glass everywhere. On the floor by the tree, like a present, sits a rounded river stone. Marie thinks it's evidence, but her mother snatches it up, stalks outside and chucks it into the yard, comes back in, still livid, and calls her father—not Russ.

He gets there before the cops, bringing his toolbox and a sheet of plywood, and stays after they've left.

"You guys gonna be all right now? I can sleep on the couch if you want."

"No," her mother says. "It was probably just kids."

"I offered."

"You did. Thank you."

"Anytime."

"Your father's a good man," her mother says when he's gone, and though she's called him an asshole as recently as last week, Marie understands. When it comes to her parents, she tells herself she has no expectations, but it's good to see them getting along. The problem is she always wants more. The same with Angel. Sometimes she thinks it would be easier if she quit hoping.

The next night, at five to eight, they're at her grandmother's, sitting around the kitchen table, playing rummy, watching the clock above the sink tick off the minutes.

"Don't tell her about the window," her mother says.

"I won't," Marie says, because her mother's already reminded her twice. They're only supposed to talk about happy things, like the tree. All of Marie's questions will have to wait.

When the phone finally rings, it still surprises her.

The recorded voice is so loud that she can hear it across the table. "You have a collect call from Westerly Correctional Facility."

"I'll accept," her mother says. "Hang on, babe, let me put you on speaker. Try it now."

"Hey, everybody," Angel says, sounding squelchy and muffled, like she's underwater.

"Your sister's here."

"Hey," Marie says, leaning closer to the phone.

"Hey," Angel says. "What's up?"

Marie's wanted this ever since she went away. She's had days to prepare—there's Christmas, and cutting down the tree with her father, and her grandmother showing her how to make chowder—but all she can think of is the window and the stone on the floor and who might have thrown it.

"Nothing," she says. "What's up with you?"

The Parrishes already have a lawyer—a whole firm, actually, because they can afford it. They no longer talk to Carol. One of DozierAllyn's minions calls to see if she's retained counsel, making it clear they're not on the same side, if they ever were, and she has to admit she hasn't. The bail hearing is a week away and she feels like she's falling behind.

The sole lawyer she's hired in her life handled her divorce and wasn't worth the money. The ones Wes knows aren't the right kind, meaning they only deal with people like him. Frank's no help, her mother still curses the ambulance chasers that botched her father's workman's comp claim, and she's not going to ask her colleagues at the Elms. Knowing her situation, Reverend Ochs refers her to a nonprofit that does pro bono work, but when she calls, they can't guarantee who'll be assigned to her case, which doesn't sound all that different from the public defender's office. Even if it bankrupts her, she's not going to bet her daughter's life on the luck of the draw.

The one person who could help is Russ, but asking him is complicated. She's not sure how much she should rely on him. They haven't been out since the police searched the house, as if they're on a break. If he dropped her, she wouldn't blame him, and she's afraid that asking him to be part of these decisions might scare him away. She doesn't want him to pay for anything, and worries that he may think she's fishing. At the same time, she can't deny there's a small part of her that hopes he'll save her, because no one else will.

She calls him after work, sitting on the corner of her bed in her scrubs, kneading her feet.

"First," she says, "I'm just asking for your advice as a friend. Feel free to say no."

"No. Kidding. Of course. Anything."

"I don't have a lot of experience with lawyers," she says.

As she explains her situation, she feels false, as if she's putting on an act, appealing to his masculine expertise to get what she wants. She has so little pride left. Why does it bother her to admit what she doesn't know?

"I'll ask around," he says, as if she's looking to borrow a snowblower. "I eat dinner with some guys who used to be lawyers. I'll pick their brains."

"That would be a big help."

"How are you doing?"

"A little overwhelmed."

"I bet. Anything you need, let me know."

"Thank you for offering."

"I'm serious. I'm not doing anything constructive here."

"Watch out," she says, "I may take you up on it," and when she gets off, she's relieved. Why does she always underestimate him?

Two hours later he calls back with a name: Howard Berman.

"He's not cheap, but they say he's worth it."

"I don't think any of them are cheap."

"He did the one in Matunuck where the boy killed his mother with the bat."

"I remember that. What happened to him?"

"I don't know, but he takes on these kinds of cases."

What kinds of cases? she wants to ask, but he's doing her a favor, and she can only thank him.

She googles Howard Berman and discovers the boy was not guilty by reason of insanity, a defense she doesn't think they can use, but not guilty is not guilty. Everything else about him looks fine, and at break the next morning she calls and makes an appointment.

When she tells Russ, she feigns helplessness, saying she's nervous about meeting him. She worries that she won't know the right questions to ask.

"Do you want me to come with you?" Russ asks, and so they go together, leaving out Frank entirely.

Howard Berman is at least seventy-five, and a giant, a good foot taller than Russ, his hair dyed an improbable root beer brown that makes it look like a toupee. In college he was a basketball star at URI; on the wall, among his diplomas, are pictures of him from his playing days. He gestures to the two chairs across from his desk with his massive hands. On his blotter he has a file he pats to show he knows the case.

"What kind of person is your daughter?" he asks, and Carol's stumped. She'd thought they were going to talk about the hearing. "Is she quiet, is she loud? Is she athletic? Does she have a strong personality? Is she a leader, a follower?"

"She's strong but not a leader. She's not quiet but she's not loud either. She's a good kid. She's on the volleyball team, she takes care of her sister. She's never been in any trouble before, not even a speeding ticket."

"Any anger issues?"

She glances at Russ, who's taking notes, because he knows their troubles. "Every teenager has anger issues."

"What about the boyfriend? What's he like?"

"He's a stoner. Good-looking, rich. I think he might sell a little weed. He drives one of those souped-up cars and plays guitar, that's about it."

"Ever been in any trouble that you know of?"

"Not that I know of."

"And they've been together for three years."

She has to count back. "Yes."

"I'm going to be honest with you," he says, leaning closer, as if in confidence. "Your daughter is looking at significant prison time. I'll do everything I can to minimize that time, but I want to be up front with you."

"What if she didn't do it?" she says.

"Oh, we're going to plead not guilty, that's not a question. His people will too. I've worked with them, good people. We'll try to separate the cases and shoot for reasonable doubt. That's the best we can hope for, but it's also the highest risk. I'm willing to take our chances, depending on how things play out, but unless I'm missing something—and I've been doing this a long time—at the end of the day the best we're going to do here is some kind of plea deal. And there are all kinds of plea deals. I'm not saying she has to roll over on him."

"I don't think she'd do that."

"Probably not, if she's been with him that long, but she needs to be aware that it's an option, because I guarantee his people are telling him the same thing. If there's a deal on the table, we want it to be ours, but like I said, there are all kinds of deals."

"So, wait," Carol says, looking to Russ for corroboration. "We don't want a trial?"

"We want it to be our *choice* to go to trial or not. If the situation isn't favorable—and a lot of things can change between now and then—we want to make sure we have options in place."

"Even if she's innocent."

"*Especially* if she's innocent. A case like this is all about managing risk, so we need to cover our bases. We don't want to be surprised."

"What's 'significant' time?" Russ asks.

"Ballpark, with all the additional charges I'd expect them to tack on, being conservative, ten years to life."

"And with a plea deal?" she asks.

"It depends how the state feels about its case. I've done a number of deals with this AG I thought were fair, and I've never taken a deal for a client that I've regretted."

"Ten years?" Russ asks.

"Impossible to say until I dig in. I'd need to talk to your daughter and see everything they have before I can tell you."

"What about bail?" she asks, because they're getting too far ahead.

"First-time offender her age, bail shouldn't be a problem."

It's all she wants to hear. The rest they can figure out later. "How much do you think it'll be?"

"The schedule's fifty thousand for the charge we're already looking at. Could go up or down, depending on the judge."

"Cash or bond?" Russ asks.

"Surety. I'll have a bondsman available there. You write him a check for ten percent and she goes home with you."

In the Escalade, on the way back to her place, they're quiet, as if absorbing the news.

"What did you think of him?" Russ asks.

"It sounds like he doesn't want to try the case."

"He said he would if he thought it was the best option."

"He made it sound like it wouldn't be."

"He seemed very sharp to me. And very realistic."

"Am I not being realistic?" she asks, because, against all the evidence, she still wants to believe Angel's innocent.

"No, but he obviously knows his job. I like that he had a plan."

"I don't know. Is this the best we can do?"

"It might be."

"He's expensive." His retainer is more than she has in the bank, and that's just to take the case.

"I can help."

"I'm not asking you to."

"I know."

"I just wanted him to be more positive, I guess. It feels like we've already lost."

"I liked what he said about the bail."

"Yeah."

The hearing is in three days, and she feels rushed. She discusses the lawyer with her mother, who doesn't have an opinion but offers to help with expenses. Frank says he's heard of Berman, which is as close to an endorsement as he gets. She doesn't volunteer that Russ was there, or that he may help pay for it. Wes never returns her call, the asshole. When she talks with Angel, Angel shrugs as if one lawyer is as good as another, and Carol wants to reach across the table and shake her. It's Carol's decision to make, but how can she be certain when she doubts everything now?

Having no other choice, she hires him, afraid it's a mistake she'll have to pay for the rest of her life.

"No," Russ says. "It's the right move."

"I hope so."

The hearing is Friday morning at the county courthouse in Wakefield, twenty minutes away. Marie wants to go, but it's when she's in school, or that's the excuse Carol uses. As a consolation, she lets her help choose Angel's outfit. Berman says whatever she wears to church will work, and the two of them go through her closet, laying a plain white blouse, gray cardigan and tweed skirt on her bed, and a pair of black flats. It reminds Carol of her mother ironing her father's clothes for his funeral, the board set up in the kitchen, carefully folding his slacks and sliding them into a grocery bag tipped on its side. Carol takes the same care with Angel's, waiting till morning to zip them into a hanging bag so they won't wrinkle.

Russ is early, wearing a dark suit and tie she's never seen before, and swings by her mother's to pick her up. It's the first time they've met, a fact her mother has to remark upon. As they ride up Route 1 through Charlestown and Matunuck, she cross-examines him, establishing that his family is Quebecois, asking if he knows the Perraults and the Dulacs and the Deschenes. Carol's embarrassed, but he humors her, trying to score points. It turns out she worked with some of his cousins at the Line & Twine.

"It really is a small world," her mother says.

"Too small," Carol says.

They need to be there an hour early to drop her clothes off, but when they turn in, the reporters are waiting for them, cameramen shooting through the windows as Russ parks. He runs interference, shielding her mother with the hanging bag. That strategy would work except the side door they're supposed to enter is locked. The swarm follows them around front, bombarding Carol with questions, using Angel's name as if they know her. She's learned not to answer, not to smirk or duck her head as if she's trying to hide, but her mother's new to the game, and begins swearing at them.

"Stop," Carol says, trying to keep her voice even. "That's what they want. Just ignore them."

It's too late, of course. No matter what her mother does now, she'll be on the news, bleeped out, for all her friends to see. Somehow that will also be Carol's fault.

The holding cells are in the basement, but they're not allowed to visit with her. They hand the clothes over to a matron stationed behind thick Plexiglas. She disappears down a hallway and returns with Howard Berman, who has to wait for her to buzz him out.

A politician, he shakes hands with her mother first. "Is this everyone?" he asks, as if he expected more.

"My ex-husband said he was coming, but he's driving himself."

"You're going to be in the front row on the right. You'll see the table. I think we're in good shape. No surprises, knock wood."

"Is there anything we need to do?" she asks.

"You've already done it by showing up."

There's a coffee shop off the lobby, but it's full of reporters chattering and tapping at their laptops like it's any other day. They congregate in the hallways, their eyes following her as she passes. The only safe place is the courtroom itself—smaller than she expected, a windowless box on the second floor paneled in dark wood. Empty, with its wide aisle and raised judge's bench, it reminds her of a church. She wants to sit directly behind Angel, but the table has three chairs. They take their places and wait.

Her phone has a message from Frank: *c u there*. Unfairly, she thinks it would be like him to be late, but the message was ten minutes ago, so he has some time. She's flanked by her mother and Russ. It'll be interesting to see who he sits beside—if he sits with them at all.

"I should have brought my knitting," her mother says.

"I don't think that would be a good look," Carol says.

"You're right, I didn't think of that."

She's cleaning out her inbox when the doors behind them clank open. She turns to see who it is, expecting a few reporters slipping in early to grab a good seat. Instead, it's a young couple with a baby, stopping in the aisle and casting around the room as if they might be in the wrong place, and beside them, squat and brown, dressed in mourning, her face unmistakable, as if she's stepped out of the TV, the girl's mother.

Why didn't the lawyer warn her?

Out of natural curiosity, or maybe as penance, more than once Carol's visited the girl's Facebook page, sitting with a last glass of wine after Marie's gone to bed, scrolling through the tributes, watching the videos of her opening Christmas presents and building sandcastles, the same innocent memories she has of Angel and Marie. What would she do if she lost one of her girls? She may be losing Angel, but it's not the same. She'd never say she understands what the woman's going through, and yet, deep down she believes the two of them share a connection.

Sitting in the front row as they approach, she feels exposed. The girl's mother is weeping, dabbing at her eyes with a handkerchief, the daughter supporting her elbow. Carol thinks it only decent that she acknowledge her loss and tell her she's sorry, one mother to another.

She pats Russ's leg and he stands, letting her slide by.

When the mother realizes what she's trying to do, she stops walking. She stands planted in the aisle, glowering at her. Carol raises an open hand to show she means well, but the mother shakes her head and shoos her with the handkerchief, as if through with her foolishness.

The daughter—taller than Angel—steps between them and gestures for Carol to move aside.

"Tell your mother I'm sorry," she says, but the daughter turns away without a word, blocking her so her mother can pass, and Carol understands that this is the bond they share: like Angel, she will always be her enemy.

They sit in their separate rows, behind their separate tables, their men on the end.

"You tried," her mother says, and Carol wishes she'd be quiet.

Gradually the reporters file in, filling the seats along the back wall, murmuring whenever the baby fusses.

Frank makes it with time to spare, wearing a dress shirt she bought for him a decade ago tucked into his best jeans. Rather than join them in the front row, he takes the seat behind her.

"Sorry," he whispers.

"No, I'm glad you could make it."

"Is everything okay?" Meaning, has she found a way to pay the bondsman?

"We're good."

There must be a secret elevator, because a door in the paneling opens and Howard Berman emerges, followed by Angel in her church clothes, her hair pulled back in a low ponytail, her only makeup some blush. Carol's grown so used to seeing her in her prison scrubs that the transformation's shocking. She could be in eighth grade. As the lawyer escorts her to the table, Angel nods to them, then takes the seat directly in front of her. While he lays out his papers, Carol reaches across the rail and squeezes her elbow. Angel glances back and pats her hand as if to say everything's going to be okay.

The judge enters, the bailiff calling them to rise.

After they've waited so long, the hearing takes no time at all. Berman was right. The prosecutor wants her bond pushed up to sixty thousand, but Berman argues that as a first-time offender with roots in the community, she's not a flight risk, and the judge keeps it at fifty. He raps his gavel and they're done.

Carol hugs Angel across the rail, a little teary, breathing in the scent of her hair. She wants to hold on to her longer, but she has to go with the bailiff. Russ and Frank both shake Berman's hand as if he's gotten her off. Once they pay the clerk, it'll take an hour or two for her to be processed. Fifty thousand dollars. It's more money than she's ever had in her life. The bondsman's waiting for them downstairs.

The room clears out, the reporters scattering. In the celebration, Carol's lost track of the girl's family, and finds them in the hallway, the mother speaking to a TV crew shining a blinding spotlight, the daughter with the baby standing by her side the way she did when the girl was missing. As Carol passes, the mother raises her voice. "The people who did this to my child don't have to answer to me," she says, "they have to answer to God," and while Carol wants to protest, she knows she's right.

Ahead, another cameraman is walking backwards, trying to catch her reaction, and Russ cuts in front of him, ruining his shot. Not to be outdone, Frank uses his broad shoulders to clear a path for her through the crowd. Why do the men in her life always think they need to rescue her?

The reporters aren't allowed to follow them down to the basement. An hour later, after Russ writes the check and Angel's finally released, they're still lurking, mobbing the side door like autograph hounds. They want Angel, they don't care about anyone else, and while Russ brings the Escalade around, making a show of parking as close as he can to the stairwell, Frank sneaks her out the front to his truck. It feels like a victory, like the day, and though Carol knows it's only temporary, and expensive, she's just happy to have Angel back. They can worry about the future later. For now, she's free.

Angel hasn't talked to him since they were arrested, and after what happened the last time, her mother won't let her have her phone or her laptop. She can't go back to school and she can't stay home alone, so she wastes the days at her grandmother's, still a prisoner, looking for ways to escape.

He's out now. His bail was higher than hers, which the lawyer says is a good sign. He's never met Myles, and doesn't care if he's guilty or not. The trial's like a game. The idea is to blame everything on him because he's the guy—bigger, stronger. She imagines him stuck at home, trying to call her, leaving message after message, convinced she's ghosting him, or worse. Every time she meets with the lawyer, he says she doesn't have to flip on Myles to cut a deal, so why does he keep mentioning it?

That's what her mother wants.

"He doesn't care about you," she says, "otherwise he wouldn't have done this."

Her mother's so wrong that she's tempted to tell her the truth, despite the promise they made each other that night, wants to laugh in her face and say, "He only did it for me."

Marie's curious but afraid to ask her straight-out. After school, the two of them share the couch at her grandmother's, watching her old standard-definition TV, the picture blurry, as if it's being broadcast from the past. Marie wants to know if it was cold in jail, how the food was, what the other girls were like, but stops short of what put her there, as if Angel might be offended, which she appreciates. She doesn't want to lie to Marie. Right now she needs her, the little spy. The middle school library has computers, and Marie loves a secret.

"Will you do something for me?" Angel asks when their grandmother goes upstairs. She whispers so Marie has to lean closer.

"What?" Marie whispers back, intrigued.

Angel can't imagine his parents taking his phone, but who knows. Sometimes during the day she pictures him cruising by their house in the Volvo, looking for her. She still thinks they should have run away. They still can. It doesn't have to be Fiji, it could be California. She's so sick of her mother telling her how she needs to be more grateful to Russ for paying her bail.

If Myles pulled up right now and opened the door for her, she'd get in and never look back.

MU, she writes on the last page of Marie's notebook. *Forever, A*

"That's it?"

"It's just a test."

"I can't send it until lunchtime," Marie says, and like that they're a team again.

They make dinner together, their grandmother checking on their progress like a head chef. No one has to say they're catering to her. Swiss steak, clam fritters, chicken à la king—every night since she's been home they've had one of her favorites, as if she may never get them again. And it's true, the food at the jail was crap. Sometimes she forgets she has to go back, and then she remembers that she may never see him again. It hasn't even been two weeks and she's already lost.

Her mother shows up in her scrubs, apologizing for being late, and they eat at the dining room table, talking about Marie's paper for English class and Aunt Mil's cataracts and the neighbors' garbage can blowing down the street.

"Ready for our big meeting Thursday?" her mother asks her, as if it fits with the rest of their small talk.

"I guess."

"What's it about?" her grandmother asks, because she has to know everything.

"He's just going to give us an update on where we are," her mother says.

"And where are we?"

Nowhere, Angel wants to say, but lets her mother explain how discovery works. The prosecution has to share whatever evidence they have so they can build a defense against it. The whole process is pointless, Angel thinks, a maze of technicalities. She's sorry, but nothing's going to change what happened. Accident or not, she knows she's supposed to feel remorse, but when she's being honest with herself, she has to admit a part of her wanted the little bitch dead. There's something wrong with her. In her lowest moments she locks her door and kneels by her bed like a child, afraid she's beyond God's mercy.

Because they cooked, her mother does the dishes, her grandmother drying them with a cigarette in her mouth, dropping ashes on the floor. Marie wants to get home so she can watch her shows and crams her books into her backpack, zips up her puffy coat. They all gather in the front hall. Kissing Angel goodbye, her grandmother holds on to her as if this might be the last time, and Angel can only stand there until she lets go.

"See you tomorrow," her grandmother says. "Sweet dreams."

Outside it's freezing and clear, the stars glimmering. After being cooped up all day, Angel breathes in the clean air, watching the sky, surrendering to the feeling of infinite space. How is the world still beautiful?

Home, first thing, her mother turns the tree on, and the outside lights, blinking like a marquee. She hasn't had the front window fixed, but she's hung mistletoe and set out bowls with red and green M&M's Marie devours by the handful, and there are Santas everywhere. Like Chevy Chase, she's obsessed with making this the best Christmas ever, as if Angel needs another reminder that she won't be home next year. The Advent calendar on the mantel is like a ticking clock. Every day she's one day closer to not being here, and that's fine. She'll give them Christmas. She just wants to see him one more time.

Marie says goodnight, giving them each a kiss. While her mother hunches over her laptop and sips her wine, Angel flips through the channels.

"Five years with time off," her mother says. It's become a habit of hers, searching the web for plea deals like she's pricing used cars. "I think five years is pretty good."

She knows her mother's just trying to wear her down so she'll accept the inevitable. What bothers her is that she's not being realistic. They're not going to offer her five years unless she testifies against him. After Thursday, her mother will have to see that.

"It's better than ten," Angel says.

"That's right."

"Or twenty."

"That's not funny."

"No," she says, "it's not. I'm going to bed. I'm tired."

Her mother sighs. "I wish you'd think about what you're doing."

"I am."

"No, you're not. You're thinking about him. You need to take care of yourself."

"I'm not going to say he did something he didn't do."

"I'm not asking you to. Just tell them what happened."

"I'm just doing what Mr. Berman told me to do. Isn't that why we're paying him, to tell us what to do?"

"You're not paying him."

"Neither are you, your boyfriend is."

"Go," her mother says, pointing to the stairs. "Ungrateful little shit."

"I am grateful—"

"Just go. You're pissing me off."

In bed, wallowing, she thinks it will always be her fault. The best she can hope for is to make sure Myles doesn't pay for what she's done. The honorable solution is to tell the truth. She may as well confess, like her mother wants. He can testify against her and get a better deal. Let the lawyers figure it out. She wants to call him and end all of this waiting around, but even now, drowsing, she's losing track of her logic, how it's all supposed to fit together, and in the morning the idea seems naive. Now that it's too late to save anyone, she needs to think about the consequences of her actions.

After breakfast they pile in the car, her mother dropping Marie off first, hunched like an astronaut under her backpack.

"Have a good day," her mother calls, not knowing all of Angel's hopes go with her.

Her grandmother doesn't have a computer or a cellphone, just a regular landline, one mustard-colored receiver on the wall in the kitchen, another black, old-fashioned model next to her bed. During the day, Angel cases her. After she's had her first cup of coffee, she locks herself in the upstairs bathroom, taking the crossword, and in the middle of the afternoon sometimes lies down and has a nap. That's when Angel would try it, but that's a last resort.

Marie gets out of school at three. At five till, Angel's watching the road, distracted by every passing car. The walk only takes Marie a few minutes, long enough for Angel to imagine all the possibilities. She has to stop hoping, afraid she's jinxing it.

There's Marie, finally, the tassel of her hat bobbing along the top of the neighbors' hedge. She trudges up the driveway under her backpack, in no hurry, which Angel thinks is a bad sign, unless she's messing with her. She tries to read her face, but she's looking down, caught up in her own thoughts.

Before she reaches the steps, Angel opens the storm door.

"Well?"

"I sent it."

"Did he write back?"

"I don't know," Marie says, as if that wasn't part of her job.

"Did you check?"

"You're only allowed fifteen minutes."

"Did you check at the end of your fifteen minutes?"

The way Marie pauses says it all.

"How could you not check?"

"I'm sorry. I'll check tomorrow."

"It's my fault," Angel says. "I should have told you to check."

"What's the problem?" her grandmother calls from the kitchen.

"Nothing," they both say.

She feels like they've wasted a whole day. She doesn't have time to wait for his answer, and makes her next message plain: *need to c u*

Overnight it snows enough to bury the road, delaying school, and her father swings by to plow their driveway. It's the first time she's seen him since the hearing, the two of them riding home in his truck, laughing at the stupid reporters. Her mother invites him inside for coffee, but he can't stop, so she fixes him a travel mug and—being completely obvious—asks Angel to take it out to him.

Maybe it was his idea, because he seems happy to see her.

"How are you holding up?" He has the defroster blowing, and his face is red.

"Okay, I guess."

"Your mom tells me you have a big meeting tomorrow."

So no, it was hers. "Yeah."

"Be smart, huh? Listen to your lawyer."

"I will."

"Okay. Hang in there. I love you."

"I love you too," she says, and watches him back out and wave to her before taking off.

Why is she fighting them when they all want the best for her? They don't have to tell her she's not being smart, she knows she isn't. Her problems can't be solved by their advice, no matter how well intentioned.

That afternoon Marie's early, hustling across the yard, her backpack bobbling. Her cheeks are pink, and she's panting. She says she ran all the way.

She's written his answer in purple: *mu to forever m*

Angel closes the notebook and clasps it to her chest. "Thank you. When did he send it?"

Again, Marie blanks.

"I didn't look."

"Really?" But it doesn't matter. He knows.

monday 1:30? she writes, and Marie looks at her like she shouldn't.

"Where?" Marie asks.

"He knows where."

The next afternoon, their appointment with the lawyer is at two, so by the time they're sitting down across from him, Marie's already sent Myles her message and maybe even received his reply. The idea sustains Angel as the lawyer goes over the evidence that could put her away for life. The folder is thick, full of pictures she doesn't want to see. The lawyer calls her "she," even though she's sitting right there.

They're lucky, he says. Because the body was underwater for so long, there's no useful DNA evidence. The blood found in the kitchen matches the victim's, but because all three of them were known to frequent the house, there's nothing to put her at the scene at that particular time. There is no time. It's his house. It's his car with the blood in it.

No, Angel thinks, blinking, trying to hide her surprise. They were so careful. It was probably just a drop. Or is it a trick?

"The only evidence they have against her that I can see is circumstantial. She and the victim are rivals. She has a previous run-in with the victim."

"I didn't hear about this," her mother says, turning to her.

"It's a scuffle between some teenage girls in a parking lot," the lawyer says. "Never reported, never documented, legally hearsay, inadmissible. Jury never hears it. I'm going to be honest, the phone records aren't great, the texts, but . . ." He lays his giant hand on the file. "If I'm a juror, I don't see anything here that convinces me beyond a reasonable doubt of murder."

"That's good," her mother says.

"Take murder out of the equation, and we're still looking at conspiracy murder, manslaughter, which isn't a small thing, and obstruction. I've talked with the AG's office. They think they probably have enough for the last two from the phone records and texts, and I didn't say this, but I agree. Conspiracy is very hard to prove, so they're willing to drop it if we plead to manslaughter, which I think is a better-than-fair offer."

Sitting there listening to him, Angel thinks manslaughter is right. She remembers Myles trying to get ahold of Birdy's arms, the three of them grappling on the kitchen floor, Birdy kicking her in the face, and the taste of blood, then blindly hitting her until Myles pulled her away.

"What's their offer?" her mother asks.

"Off the record, somewhere between five and seven years."

"How much of that would she have to serve?"

"With good behavior, as little as three to five."

Her mother looks to her for her opinion, hopeful, as if they've been saved. "Three to five years isn't bad."

"Five to seven years," Angel corrects her.

"Think about it and get back to me," the lawyer says. "Things can change quickly, so we want to have an answer ready for them if they put something on the table. All right?" He stands.

While her mother's shaking his hand, Angel tries to picture the blood in Myles's car. So they don't need her testimony. It should be a relief, but it only makes it worse.

"How much time will he get?" she asks.

"I wouldn't venture a guess at this point. I know they're in talks. Another reason to get back to me ASAP with your decision."

In the car, her mother doesn't understand why she's not ready to say yes, and keeps prodding her with the three to five. Angel can't say it's not fair, that at worst they deserve the same sentence. She can't say she needs to talk to him.

monday 1:30, he's written back, finally catching up, but Monday's too late. She needs to see him now.

should I take 5-7 yrs? she writes.

Marie doesn't have an opinion. "It's your life," she says, which Angel appreciates. No one else seems to understand that.

Her grandmother says she should take it. After dinner, her mother calls her father and then Russ, explaining how she'd serve only three to five with good behavior, and they both agree.

"Can I have one day to think about it?" Angel says. "It's not even official. It might not even happen."

"We need to be ready," her mother says, as if Angel wasn't there at the lawyer's with her.

"I'll be ready."

"You're not the one who needs to be ready. He needs to be ready when they call him."

"He can call me. It takes five seconds. It's not like I'm going anywhere."

"I just don't want us to miss an opportunity here," her mother says, softening. She wants her to promise they won't.

"I'll be ready," Angel says.

Friday it snows again, a dusting on the road like powdered sugar, showing tire tracks. All morning she waits for the phone to ring. When it finally does, around lunchtime, it's her mother, checking to see if she's heard anything.

"I'd let you know if I did."

"Have you thought any more about it?"

"That's all I'm doing," Angel says. "All day."

"Let me know when you decide."

"I will."

After their grilled cheese and tomato soup, her grandmother goes upstairs to lie down. It's only twelve-thirty, earlier than usual. Angel watches the clock, dreaming of Monday. She's tired of waiting, and the phone's right there, but she holds off, knowing Marie will be home soon. At two-twenty her grandmother comes down and lights up a cigarette. Angel marks the time like a jewel thief. She should have an hour, an hour and a half before she realizes she's gone.

"How was your nap?" she asks.

"Too short," her grandmother says.

She kills the last half hour baking cookies and making real hot chocolate for Marie, warming the milk till there's a skin on it, spilling cocoa powder all over the stove. She stands at the window, watching for her tassel, then goes to the door to meet her, trying to read her eyes. Marie sniffs the air and lets Angel help her off with her backpack. Normally she sits on the couch with Angel while she reads his answer, but today she joins her grandmother in the kitchen, giving Angel privacy. When she opens the notebook and flips to the very end, she sees why. There, in purple, in Marie's girly bubble letters, Myles advises her: *take it*

She claps the notebook closed as if she can make it go away. He's trying to be noble. She'll have to talk to him on Monday and see what he's thinking. He should be worried about himself. She catches herself and has to laugh. She sounds just like her mother.

At five to five, the kitchen phone rings, shocking her heart, and she's afraid this is it, it's the lawyer saying she needs to decide right now.

"Here she is," her grandmother says, handing her the phone.

"Did you hear anything?" her mother asks.

"No, did you?"

"No," her mother says, dispirited. "I guess we'll have to wait till Monday."

"I guess so," Angel says, thankful for the reprieve.

It doesn't last the evening. They're back home, Marie's already gone to bed, when her mother gets a call from the lawyer. The girl's car has been found.

"Where?" her mother asks.

She covers the mouthpiece. "He wants to know if there's anything you want to tell him about the car."

"No," Angel says, hoping they cleaned it better than they cleaned his.

"Did you hear anything more about the deal?" her mother asks. "Okay, keep us posted."

When she gets off, neither of them speaks, the Christmas lights blinking as they try to figure out what this discovery means.

"Where was it?" Angel asks, because she honestly doesn't know.

"New London. Someone set it on fire."

Good. Her hair was probably in it, her DNA.

"Should I even bother asking you what you know about it?"

"No." It's as close to a confession as she's made, and her mother shakes her head as if she can't believe the person she's become.

"Will you take the deal now?"

"Is there still a deal?"

"I don't know. He didn't sound happy. Nothing's going to happen till Monday."

All weekend the threat hangs heavy over her. Playing board games on the floor with her father and Marie, singing in church, watching the Patriots at her grandmother's, she pictures a CSI team processing the car in a brightly lit garage, tweezing her hairs from the carpet and sliding them under a microscope. She only drove it because she can't drive a stick, Myles following in the Eclipse to the Foxwoods employee park-and-ride lot, filled 24-7. The key ring had a miniature baseball bat on it, and some house keys she didn't want to think about. She gave it to him, trusting he'd get rid of the car later. Like the drum, their plan didn't work. They're amateurs—they're idiots, thinking they could get away with it. They deserve everything they get.

Ten years, twenty. Monday she just has to last till one-thirty, and she can't even do that. Around noon the phone rings, making her grandmother lower her radio.

"It's your mother," she says, to Angel's relief.

"The deal is on," her mother says. "He needs an answer. I've got him on hold."

It's the same deal as before, five to seven with the possibility of parole. She turns away from her grandmother so she can think.

"What about the car?"

"They won't get to it for a while, so now's the time."

"Can I have till the end of today?"

"Jesus Christ. No. You said you'd be ready. What's going to change by the end of the day? It's on the table, just take it."

"I did it," Angel says flatly, aware that her grandmother is listening.

"I know you did," her mother says. "It doesn't matter. He did it too."

"He didn't. It was me, the whole thing."

"Both of you did this. It doesn't matter what parts you did. That's not how the law works. It's not going to hurt him one way or the other, if that's what you're worried about. You don't have to testify, you don't have to do anything. It's a good deal, Ange."

"I know it is."

"They're not going to offer it again. Take it. Please."

The lawyer's waiting. Everyone wants her to, even Myles, and she knows he's right. Is it just pride that makes her resist? Because now she can see no practical reason not to. She won't have to testify, won't have to confess. She can plead guilty and still be true to him, keep their secret forever. They're both going away anyway.

"Okay," she says, and does what she swore she'd never do.

"That's a smart move," her grandmother says over lunch, but Angel's not so sure. She feels strange, as if she's given up something precious, and wishes she'd fought harder.

After her Lorna Doones, her grandmother climbs the stairs to her bedroom. Without the radio, the house is quiet, only the clatter of a passing snowplow. The sky is blue, the roads dry, but they're supposed to get four to six inches tonight. The forecasters are excited about a white Christmas. Angel listens for her to shut the door. It's not quite one, so she has some time, but she's impatient. She's been waiting so long.

She points her toes into her boots, turns the knob of the front hall closet like a safecracker, using two hands to remove her jacket so the hangers don't clink. Gloves, hat, sunglasses. She has a house key but won't need it. How easy it is to escape when you don't care about getting caught again.

Outside, the sun is blinding, the drifted snow glinting like mica. She eases the storm door closed behind her, tiptoes down the concrete steps as if they might creak. The people across the way have a leering blow-up Grinch in the yard and wreaths on the old barn they use for a garage. Not everyone has shoveled their walks, and she keeps to the edge of the street, where the town plows have left icy heaps. The air smells of woodsmoke, and she's glad to be out of the house, free, for a little while, of her keepers.

The village is a Christmas card, holly bushes and shaggy pines laden with snow. She crosses High Street at the crosswalk by the library, keeps on along the side of the middle school, waving in case Marie might see her. She used to play on this playground, swing on these swings. Five to seven years. Seven years ago she was eleven, another person. Who will she be when she gets out?

At the corner, she turns into Cemetery Lane. They used to go to church this way. After her grandfather died, at the start of Advent they'd walk over together and lay a wreath on his grave. She was his favorite, their first grandchild. This year she wasn't here to lay the wreath. She'll have to stop and say a prayer.

The lot of the church is empty, scraped bare, a mound of snow piled by a dumpster. No one's plowed the dirt road into the cemetery, but there's a muddy track of footprints down one rut. The headstones are caked, their pedestals outlined in white, the only color the miniature flags remembering veterans. Deer have left meandering trails between the rows. With the leaves down, the view goes all the way to the river. Swallows wing across the open space, dipping and swerving. Below, by her grandfather's plot, some old guy in an army jacket is walking his dog. The wind must be right because she can smell his cigar from here. The slope and the snow make the footing treacherous, even with her hiking boots. As she tacks downhill, she slips and skids, almost falling. She turns her feet sideways to stop herself, digging in her edges like a skier. The man watches her, circling around to the right, keeping his distance. The dog barks, and she waves, earning a friendly wave in return, reminding her that she's in disguise.

The path through the woods is untouched, giving her the pleasure of breaking the crust with every step. The pond isn't quite frozen, it hasn't been cold enough. A gray slick of water sits atop the ice, which looks soft and rotten. She imagines walking straight out onto it and dropping through, Myles finding her floating facedown. She shakes her head at the thought. Why does she need everything to be tragic now?

There's a log the skaters use as a bench, and she clears off a spot, then makes another for him to show she has faith that he's coming. If he doesn't, she doesn't know what she'll do. Climb the hill and go home again, or maybe just stay. She feels safe here, in their special place, at peace, watching the birds weave above the treetops. She's reached the end, everything's settled, she just needs to see him once more to know it wasn't all a waste. The moon's out, a pale pill hidden in the blue. Silently, high up, a plane goes over, and she wishes she was on it. Fiji, California. She wishes they'd run away when they had the chance. Why didn't they?

She hears an engine and cocks an ear toward the church. Is it him? It doesn't sound familiar, and then it stops and she can hear the wind again, and the river. Faintly, in the distance, a car door shuts. It must be him, and she turns, craning, peering through the trees, until she sees a lean figure slouching down the hill, hands out to his sides like a snowboarder for balance.

She wants to be cool and wait for him to come to her. That lasts a minute, then she's up and running, charging back up the path through the woods, demolishing her perfect footprints. She clears the trees, laughing as he nears the bottom going too fast and loses control, flailing his arms, slipping and falling on his ass. She piles on, kissing him, biting his cheek, the two of them rolling around in the snow, finally stopping, nose to nose.

It's cold but they don't get up. It's like lying on a giant white bed. She takes her gloves off so she can hold his face.

"Oh my God, what happened to your hair?"

"It's for court."

"I'm sorry."

"How bad is it?"

"It's adorkable. You look like you're in third grade."

"That's creepy."

"No, you are," she says, and kisses him, rests her face on his chest, her arm across him. Hears his heart. Hers. "Let's just stay here."

"Okay."

As much as they try to ignore it, the cold seeps through their jeans, and they stand and brush the snow off each other and follow the path down to the pond. He's brought a flask of blackberry brandy. They sit on the log, sipping and trading sticky kisses. Somewhere on the slope below them, a woodpecker drills a tree trunk.

"I took it," she says.

"Good."

"I didn't want to."

"No, it's a good deal."

"What does your lawyer say?"

"I don't know, I don't even talk to her, my father does."

"You heard about the car."

"Yeah. I don't know why it took them so long. It was sitting there the whole time."

"Probably because it was in Connecticut."

"I guess. It doesn't matter, it was toasted. It was my car that fucked us."

"I think we fucked ourselves."

"True."

"We should have run away. You should have listened to me."

"You're probably right."

"We still can."

"What about your deal?"

"Fuck my deal."

"No, you need to take it."

"Then you run away."

"I'm not going to run away by myself," he says. "It wouldn't be any fun."

It's too cold to take off their clothes, but she has to have him one last time—here, where they've been happy, not in his mother's old car. She straddles him on the log, rocking, bearing down, his hands on her hips, their jeans building up friction until he groans and sags back, releasing her.

"Need a tissue?" she asks, because she's brought some.

He stands and unzips, grabs a handful of snow and cleans himself with it, making her shiver.

"Damn it," she says. "I wish I had my phone."

Do they let you use computers in prison? She'd ask but she doesn't want to bring him down.

They finish the pint, this time without kissing. The woodpecker's gone, only a few stubborn leaves rattling in the wind, the river flowing in the distance.

"My grandfather taught me how to fish here," she says.

"I know, you told me."

"You want to meet him?"

Hand in hand, they take the path back through the woods and climb the hill. The cemetery's empty, the dog walker long gone. The sun is lower, throwing shadows of obelisks across the road. She takes the fork to the right and shows him her grandfather's headstone, her grandmother's name engraved right beside his, just waiting for a date. The wreath with its red ribbon has blown over, half buried in the snow, and she sets it back on its stand before saying a prayer.

"He met my grandmother when she was seventeen."

"I met you when you were fifteen."

"I know," she says, as if that's the lesson.

She takes his hand again, leading him through the marble crosses and cabinlike mausoleums to the old part of the cemetery, hemmed in by crooked sections of spiked wrought-iron fence. Some of the headstones go back to colonial days, slate tablets acned with lichen, their ornate lettering faint, smoothed away by rain. BELOVED WIFE, they say, BELOVED HUSBAND. She envies these lucky couples, together for eternity, just as she mourns the children taken too early. It must be two-thirty, but she doesn't hear the buses lining up at the middle school. Marie will be home soon. Her grandmother's probably already called her mother, who's probably driving around town, frantic. Angel feels bad for scaring her, but unlike the lovers surrounding them, joined forever, this is all the time they have. They're not leaving until someone comes for them, and so they go on, strolling through the rows like a pair of ghosts, trying to say goodbye.

The Far Side of Providence

When my sister was first in prison, we used to go see her every weekend. She was in Cranston ACI, up I-95, just below Providence. Russ drove us, my mother sitting in front beside him, watching for cops, my grandmother in back with me. We went through the metal detectors, putting our phones and our rolls of quarters for the vending machines in the little bin. For safety, we had to be seated before they brought her in. There were no chairs there, only modular cafeteria tables bolted to the floor. We sat with Angel for fifty minutes, eating Fritos and drinking Diet Cokes, knowing that somewhere guards were watching us on banks of TVs. We asked how she was doing, and what she needed, and at the end of the visit we were allowed to stand and give her a hug. She smelled different to me—because of the crappy soap, my mother said, but I didn't think that was it.

"She looked good," my grandmother said on the way home, but as the months passed, it was clear she wasn't. She was taking antidepressants and gaining weight. She was seeing a counselor and getting her GED, but didn't tell us much about her life inside. She never said a word about Myles, with whom, as part of her sentence, she was forbidden to have contact. We weren't supposed to mention his name, as if she might forget him, which I thought was silly. What else was she supposed to think about?

He ended up getting less time than she did, thanks to his lawyers. The forensic investigator who processed his car had tampered with some DNA samples in another case, and the judge threw out the blood evidence. Myles took an Alford plea, not admitting guilt, and was sentenced to two to four years.

"It's because they have money," my mother said.

"Money's not enough," my father said. "This is Rhode Island. You have to know someone."

The Parrishes sold their beach house and moved away. The listing was online, complete with a virtual tour. There was the garage, there was the kitchen, there was the master bedroom with its fireplace and view of Block Island off the deck. The website didn't mention the murder. Eventually they reduced the price to $2.5 million, and took $1.8, a fact that made my mother happy when she read it in the *Sun*, as if we would ever have that much money.

On the weekends he didn't have me, my father saw Angel, but his schedule was irregular. He was dating a widow named Helene he'd met at AA. "She wants to save him," my mother scoffed, as if it was a waste of time, but Helene stood by him when he eventually relapsed, earning my mother's respect. After Russ and my mother's other suitors, I resented Helene as another intruder. Our visits were strained, and I missed Angel. My father was living with Helene in her townhouse in Stonington, so I no longer slept on his pullout couch or ate at the Chinese place. My room had been her daughter's, who was now a college professor in Maine. In the morning I'd wake up surrounded by pictures of strangers, and instead of my father's waffles, Helene would say there were bagels in the fridge.

With just the two of us, my mother and I didn't need as much space, and to save money and look after my grandmother, we moved back in with her, storing Angel's stuff in the basement. That fall I started high school, the bus taking me by our old place, empty now. The Tidwells were the only tenants left on that stretch. Sometimes I'd see Brookie standing in their window, but one morning as we passed I noticed a hunter's-orange CONDEMNED sign plastered to their front door. For months I watched for their car, but I never saw it again, and in the spring a crew from the highway department demolished the entire line of houses to widen the road.

In school, though I was nothing like Angel, I was known as the killer's little sister, a mark of shame only made worse by my need to please my teachers. I didn't suddenly become her, as I'd once wished, strong and confident with a wicked tongue. I remained the tubby little grade-grubber who loved anime and peanut butter cups. Three years straight I earned a letter in forensics. When I finally did get asked out on a date, it was by a teammate whose dream, at sixteen, was to clerk for a Supreme Court justice. He was my boyfriend for almost two years until he made the mistake of asking about Angel's case. I'm sure he didn't know why we broke up.

My sister's lawyer was right, she didn't serve her whole sentence. She made parole before I graduated, and was there to watch me walk across the stage, something she never got to do herself. She was changed when she came out, quieter, her sharp edges filed away by her medication. She rarely laughed or swore, and wasn't interested in living with us. As far as we knew, she wasn't in touch with Myles. The conditions of her parole said she had to remain in the state, but instead of coming back to Ashaway, she settled in Pawtucket, on the far side of Providence, as far away as she could get, legally. With my mother's encouragement, she studied to become a radiology technician and landed a job at a hospital there, where she met a surgical intern. When he completed his residency, they got married and moved to the suburbs of Baltimore and had a boy and a girl, making my mother a grandmother, and me Aunt Marie.

My first year out of college, while I was doing my student teaching at the middle school, my grandmother suffered a massive stroke. When it became clear she would never get out of rehab, my mother arranged for her to live with Aunt Mil on the second floor of the Elms. Like a long-married couple dying within hours of each other, they lapsed into comas on the same day, Aunt Mil outliving her by three weeks. For the first time since she'd left the state, Angel came home for our grandmother's funeral, flying in with the children. The husband was too busy. When she couldn't make it back for Aunt Mil's, we understood.

With nothing to keep her there anymore, my mother finally retired from the Elms and moved to Florida with Russ, leaving me my grandmother's house. Soon after, as if following suit, my father and Helene decamped for the White Mountains of New Hampshire, where, as he constantly reminds me, there's no state income tax. He's been sober ten years now and just bought a new truck, which he uses to plow their mile-long driveway.

I'm proud of my family and how we didn't quit. If we haven't entirely reinvented ourselves, we've moved on to new lives—all except me. I teach English at the middle school, and still love *To Kill a Mockingbird*. My room overlooks the cemetery, and if I poke my head out the window I can see my grandparents' stone, complete now. I know the rumors my students whisper about me, that I'm cursed like my sister. It happens every fall. I live alone, and when the leaves begin to turn and my neighbors decorate their porches with jack-o'-lanterns and black cats, the children treat my grandmother's house like it's haunted, daring their friends to ring the doorbell as if I'm a witch.

I'm no witch, and no spinster. I'm not my sister. I live alone by choice, by temperament. I can't imagine ever killing for love, though many times when I was younger I thought I'd die of it, and once, wanting a person I couldn't have, tried to end my life. I was older than my sister was that fall, and in pain. If I'd succeeded, I would have destroyed more lives than my own, and I'm glad that I didn't, even if I couldn't appreciate it at the time.

I keep up with Birdy's mother on social media. She's trying to get the high school to dedicate the new all-purpose field to Birdy. As an alumna, I clicked on the link to sign the petition, but it's so long ago now. I hope she'll see my name and know I haven't forgotten.

Having escaped, my family can't understand why I stay in Ashaway. They don't like to talk about that fall, as if it's ancient history. To me it's always fresh, eternal as the first day of school, new students spreading old rumors, whispers of a mad sister, and if I ever forget my own role in it—the needy keeper of secrets—I'm reminded by the cold nights and the lingering scent of woodsmoke. I still have the notebook. Sometimes, alone by the fire with a glass of wine, I'll pull it out and witness them making their plans in my childish handwriting and remember what it's like to want someone that much.

The time I was the most hopeless, I tried to become nothing. I wrote a note to the one who'd never be mine, blaming myself. I thought I'd died, but even then I wasn't free. All my life I thought I'd change into a different person, someone honest and brave, not the old Marie who was afraid of spiders and cried when my sister picked on me. For a long time I wanted to be anonymous. Now I sleep in my grandmother's bed and grease her skillet, and when I go out to rake the leaves or bring in a load from the woodpile, I wear my grandfather's barn coat. There will always be those who hate me for my name. Whenever I'm tempted to leave, I only have to drive by the Line & Twine or stand at the window of my classroom to know where I belong. Who else will remember what happened back then? Who else will tell our story?

My mother is gone.

My father is gone.

My sister is gone.

I am the only one now.

Acknowledgments

Grateful thanks to my trusty first line of readers for their honesty and generosity:

Paul Cody

Lamar Herrin

Michael Koryta

Margot Livesey

Trudy O'Nan

Alice Pentz

Susan Straight

Luis Urrea

Sung J. Woo

Special thanks to Megan Abbott and Andre Dubus III, and to Paul Tremblay and Jennifer Brehl for their early support of *Ocean State*, and to Arthur and Danielle Gobeille for their help with the intricacies of Rhode Island's many dialects. Thanks to Paul Slovak for being my champion at Viking. As always, for their efforts to put my books into readers' hands, my everlasting gratitude to David Gernert, Rebecca Gardner, Ellen Goodson Coughtrey, Will Roberts, Anna Worrall and Nora Gonzalez at the Gernert Company, and to Sylvie Rabineau, Carolina Beltran and Jack Beloff at WME. Thanks also to Maureen Klier for her keen mind and sharp eyes. And to Morgan Entrekin and Sara Vitale and Peter Blackstock and Emily Burns and Elisabeth Schmitz and Judy Hottensen and Julia Berner-Tobin and Andrew Unger at Grove Atlantic, thank you all so much for believing in *Ocean State* and giving me a new home. It's good to be back downtown.